Ordinary Wonders
A Fantasy Short Story Collection

Sandra Ulbrich Almazan

Solar Unicorn Publishing

Sandra Ulbrich Almazan/Solar Unicorn Publishing
www.sandraulbrichalmazan.com

Publisher's Note: This is a work of fiction. Names, characters, places, and incidents are a product of the author's imagination or are used factiously.

Book Layout © 2017 BookDesignTemplates.com

Ordinary Wonders/ Sandra Ulbrich Almazan. -- 1st ed.

ISBN 978-1-944437-13-8

Table Of Contents

Introduction 7

Letters to Psyche 9

The Owl and the Spider's Son 25

Silver Rain 30

Bugged Out at the Museum 42

Caps in Red and Gray 46

Blood for Sap, Sap for Blood 58

Henry's Harness 75

But Not Today 93

Last Locomotive from Wistica 106

To Name the Anilink 120

Jenna's Rosebush 147

Other Works by Sandra Ulbrich Almazan 168

About the Author 169

Introduction

Although I prefer writing novels, short stories present a challenge. When you're limited to 5,000 words or less, it's critical to make each one count. Plotting must be tight. And if you're required to do all this while finding a compelling take on a theme, so much the better.

The following stories span a significant part of my writing career. The oldest is "Letters to Psyche," featuring two famous romantic couples: Cupid and Psyche and Romeo and Juliet. The first version of that story was written sometime in the mid-to-late 1990s. The newest is "Caps in Red and Gray," which was written during the summer of 2019. Ironically, this story is a throwback to my days of writing Beatles fanfiction, imaging the Fab Four as not quite human. "Letters to Psyche" and "Silver Rain" have been previously indie-published by me as eBooks. "Bugged Out at the Museum" was written for an anthology called *Indie Writers Monthly*. It was inspired by my family's visits to the Field Museum for their annual Members Nights. "The Owl and the Spider's Son," a retelling of Athena and Arachne's weaving contest, was written for an animal-themed issue (April 2018) of the webzine *Enchanted Conversations*. "Silver Rain" was inspired by a rainy day and features a woman who sees the truth yet yearns for illusions. "Blood for Sap, Sap for Blood" is a prequel for a forthcoming urban fantasy trilogy (tentative series title: Magic of Madison) about dryads on the University of Wisconsin-Madison campus. "Henry's Harness" is also set in Madison, Wisconsin and was partly inspired by Old Abe, a captive bald eagle that was a mascot for Wisconsin troops during the Civil War. It was first published in the anthology: *MCSI: Magical Crime Scene Investigation*s in August 2018.

The second half of this book is a series of four short stories originally published as a digital collection called *Young Seasons*. *Young Seasons* is a collection of short stories featuring the four heroines of my Season Avatars series: Gwen, Jenna, Ysabel, and Kay. These stories feature them as children and teenagers and are set between *Seasons' Beginnings* and *Scattered Seasons.*

If you enjoy these stories, please check out the list of my other works at the end of this collection. Happy reading!

Best,

Sandra Ulbrich Almazan

Letters to Psyche

My Dearest Psyche,

I must be away from home for a few years. Business in the mortal world detains me. Don't worry; I shall resolve it soon.

Love,

Cupid

My Dearest Psyche,

I admit I didn't want to tell you more about the business that keeps me on Earth. However, my mother has it all wrong. Why is she still refusing to accept our marriage? We just celebrated our thousandth anniversary—or was it our twelve hundredth? I'm not on Earth to dally with a mortal, the way Jupiter would. One of the love matches I arranged has gone wrong, and I've been cursed with being parted from you until I set it right.

I can see you now, raising your perfectly arched eyebrows in surprise. How can the curse of a mortal affect a god? Jupiter's blood runs in both the Montague and Capulet families of Verona—not much, but enough to draw his attention. Giovanni and Elisabeth, the two lovers who were supposed to unite these families, are dead, and Jupiter must blame me.

It wasn't supposed to be like this. They'd already pledged themselves to each other. Giovanni gave her a ring he'd had made for her, a gold ring with a dove on each side of a heart-shaped ruby. Elisabeth in turn yielded him her most prized possession: her maidenhead. Giovanni planned to ask her father for her hand, and permission seemed certain, so why wait?

Perhaps Mercury was in a trick-playing mood, for before Giovanni could approach the head of the Capulets, he was sent on a long trading voyage. Meanwhile, Elisabeth missed her woman's flow. When she could no longer hide the truth from her family, they locked her in her room, allowing her only bread and water, until she confessed Giovanni's name. His family denied the charge, and when Elisabeth showed them the ring Giovanni had given her, they said truthfully they'd never seen it before.

In the middle of this, Giovanni, ignorant of what had happened, returned home. Elisabeth's three brothers surrounded him at the dock and forced him to fight all of them at once. Against such odds, he had no chance, especially when the youngest brother lied that Elisabeth had rejected him. Several sword thrusts followed those lethal strokes to the heart, and Giovanni fell lifeless. The brothers didn't even clean their swords before they invaded their sister's chambers with the news that her hated seducer was dead. She stared at them for a few moments before collapsing with a shriek.

What was I doing while this took place? Why, matching other pairs of lovers; you know I never have time to watch what happens to them after the first prick of lust. I was in the middle of shooting a youth when Elisabeth's first curse crashed into me, causing me to misfire. I thought it was a fluke until several more curses hit me with enough force to make me turn visible. Luckily, I became transparent and rushed to her bedchamber before the youth noticed me.

I didn't recognize Elisabeth; she was bone-thin with her wavy hair clipped short. I gleamed what had happened when the Christian priest came to hear her confession. Once he left the room and took his faith with him, I allowed myself to appear. She was close enough to death to keep my presence secret, and she didn't seem surprised to see me.

"I grieve for your loss, my lady," I told her. "It is my task to unite your houses as an example of love, not drive them apart."

"But if we were your example, why didn't you help us?" she whispered.

"I only spark love, my lady. Once it catches fire, it's up to the couple to keep it burning. How can I focus on one couple when there are so many others who need me?"

"Have you no pity for us humans, Cupid?" Her eyes appeared smudged in their sockets. "The poets say even you were pricked by your own arrow. Why do you allow so many obstacles in the path of true love?"

A pox on the poets, my dearest, for revealing what should have been kept secret. As Elisabeth spoke, I remembered eavesdropping as my mother tasked you with sorting seeds, fetching golden fleece, and even sending you to Hades. How I had to sneak around to find sympathetic helpers for you. Even with them on our side, we nearly lost each other. But would we have realized how much we needed each other if we had not been parted for a while? Nothing worth winning was ever gained easily, but greedy mortals always demand the gods make their paths as smooth as silk. So I answered her as Athena had advised us, with the words, "It is the wisdom of the gods, Lady."

"Wisdom, Cupid, or a wish to keep us blind?"

This was arrogance I would not tolerate. I was about to leave when she coughed herself into a spasm, enough to make me pity her.

She beckoned me closer. "Cupid, God of Love, I pray you hear my final request."

Foolishly, I indulged her. I could feel Jupiter's strength in her blood. Listening to her would be a favor to our supreme god, nothing more. But when I stood by her bed, she gathered all her will and jammed her lover's ring on my finger.

"If you believe the houses of Montague and Capulet should be united, then I vow in Jupiter's name never to let it happen, to spite you." She spat pink froth at me, enough blood in it to put binding behind her words. "You will not see your wife or any of the other gods until Giovanni's house and mine know enduring love."

Shocked, I tried to pull away, but death had claimed her. The ring stuck to me as if it had been dipped in honey.

I tried, my love, I tried to remove it. I swam in the ocean; I held my hand over flame. But I can't approach Vulcan's forge or Mount Olympus. It appears I am condemned to wander the Earth until this curse is broken. Don't fear for me, beloved; nothing on Earth can harm me. But since I can't appeal to Jupiter myself, could you bring him this letter and plead my case before him? Surely he will lift Elisabeth's curse when he hears my tale.

Write me soon, and send me wisdom how to deal with your former race, and seal it with a kiss.

Yours eternally,

Cupid.

Dearest Psyche,

What? Jupiter wants me to remain on Earth? What could he possibly think I need to learn from mortals? He forgets who I am and what I can do to him. The next time I prick him with my arrow, he shall fall in love with a hag and approach her as a jellyfish. Let the mortals tell that tale of him!

I have left a kiss on this letter; please send me one in return.

Yours with love,

Cupid

Dearest Psyche,

A generation has passed since Elisabeth Capulet's curse parted us. I see echoes of your face–but never your perfection–in every woman I shoot. I see couples at every stage of love, together and raising their families, and it reminds me of the days our daughter, Voluptas, was young. I see old couples grown into pleasant companions. All of these lovers show me a part of what we have, and my ache for you never dies. Hopefully soon we shall be together again.

The Montagues and Capulets have fared well while I waited for a new pair of lovers to grow up. The Montagues have added another wing to their house, and the Capulets moved closer to the prince's palace. But I feel undercurrents of rivalry between the houses. Every word the patriarchs speak in public is meant to cut the other house down. The prince of Verona tolerates them more than I would in his position.

I am not sure if this is a side effect of the curse, but there are fewer members of each family in this generation. Finding suitable candidates is difficult. However, I have found a pair: Francesca Montague and Claudius Capulet. She appears to be a quiet, pious maiden, but the passion she subverts into prayer to the crucified god can easily be returned to its true purpose. Claudius is a sensual young man. If he enjoys the lady half as much as he does wine and music, they shall be happy together.

My dearest, since you know firsthand what young mortal lovers are like, advise me here. What is the best way to prevent their families from interfering with this match? Our happiness depends on the answer. Send your answer by the same dove I send to you—and send your sweet kisses too.

Missing you,

Cupid

Dearest Psyche,

Yes, I remember your sisters only too well. Such jealous creatures, not fit to clean your shoes. I don't think jealousy will be an issue here since the Capulet and Montague families have shrank so much. Still, the more who know about love when it is most tender and vulnerable, the more likely it is that love will be torn out of the hearts where it needs to grow. If Francesca and Claudius could become invisible, or clothe themselves in darkness so no one else could see them, it would give them a chance.

A pity I cannot commission a pair of magical items for these lovers from Vulcan. However, there may be a way for them to share my gift of invisibility. Hopefully soon I will be able to report a successful union between them–and celebrate our reunion by ravishing you.

Yours longingly,

Cupid

Dearest Psyche,

Francesca and Claudius' affair is progressing nicely. Soon this curse will be broken.

As you may recall, I decided to assist this pair by helping them hide their love from the world. To do this, I had to sacrifice a feather from each wing. You know how much that hurts. At least the pain faded after a few days; my heart hasn't stopped aching for you. Since I couldn't visit Vulcan, I had to rely on a human jeweler to craft a pair of dove brooches for me. Each bird bore one of my feathers in its beak. The craftsmanship was not divine, but it was passable by mortal standards. All I had to do was wait for an opportunity to shoot the lovers.

I had my chance when the ruler of the city, Prince Escalus, died. All of the wealthy and powerful families attended his funeral. The crucified god didn't object when I slipped into his claustrophobic temple, though the weight of stone soaked in prayer made me want to flee. This Christian god may have more followers in name, but all humans long for me, even if they no longer worship me the way their ancestors did. Their adoration lets me go anywhere. I sought sanctuary in the shadows and admired the stained glass windows. Someday I'll bring you to a cathedral to see them.

The Montagues and Capulets sat on opposite sides of the church. Francesca bent her covered head in silent prayer, refusing to look up. I pricked a young child with a plain arrow until he squalled. Francesca glanced over to the Capulet's side for an instant, but that was all I needed. I put an arrow through her heart, then did the same for Claudius when he noticed her eyeing him. Neither of them paid attention to the service after that.

I gave the lovers a few days before I visited each of them in the guise of a messenger, bearing a brooch and a short note:

Who wears this pin in the service of love
Shall to others remain unseen,
But he who betrays the heart of the dove
Meets an ill end from an edge keen.

I thought that would give Francesca and Claudius a reason to keep their love a secret. Both of them experimented with the brooches before seeking each other.

They met at a fountain in the early evening, visible only to each other. The spot was perfect for lovers: the fountain shimmered with color, the water's dance provided music to mask the pair's conversation, and sweet rolls from a nearby baker fed them and the pigeons at their feet. I eavesdropped on their whispered exchanges of love and found them similar to any other pair of lovers I've shot before. Now I wait for the day they elope and Elisabeth's ring slips off my finger, freeing me to come home.

Counting the hours until I see you,

Cupid

Dearest Psyche,

Alas, I should have been in your arms by now! This letter must be as poor a substitute for me as your latest is for your sweet self. As you may have guessed, Francesca and Claudius failed us as well as themselves. Perhaps if I tell you what happened, we can figure out how I can succeed next time.

A week after the lovers first met, the ring burned my finger, warning me something was wrong. I returned to Verona in dove shape and waited on the statue gracing the lovers' fountain. Francesca arrived an hour before sunset, but Claudius didn't appear that day, or the next. Was he ill? A visit to his house proved he wasn't there either. Francesca, still wearing her brooch, paced up and down by the Capulet's gate until a couple of servants came back from the market. She slipped in with them, and I followed her.

She wandered from room to room until she came upon two maids chattering as they scrubbed the floor. "Have you seen the young master lately?" one of them asked. "He's out all day and half the night."

"He's probably at the palace," the other maid replied. "The prince's cousin is in Verona for a visit, and they say she's as lovely as she is rich."

Francesca let out a small cry, but splashing water covered the noise.

"So he's courting her?" The first maid edged closer to the door. "Think of what it would mean if he were to win her. The House of Capulet would gain ascendance over the Montagues for certain."

Francesca crept down the stairs and sped away. As soon as she returned to her home, she sent her personal attendant out of the room, flung herself on her bed, and wept. I hovered nearby, uneasy about what this development meant. Were Claudius's intentions toward the prince's cousin sincere, or was he using her to mask his intrigue with Francesca?

I flew over to the palace to see for myself. He was there, along with his father and uncle, discussing intercity politics with the prince. I sighed with relief when I saw Claudius's heart still belonged to Francesca. To make sure, I pricked him again with the same arrow I'd shot him with; it would remind him of her. Once he sought her out and apologized for his absence, all would be well.

The next day, Claudius arrived at the fountain first. He bought one sweet roll, then another, as he waited. At last, Francesca approached with slow steps.

Claudius jumped up and ran over to her. "Finally! My darling—"

She raised her hand. "Where were you the last two days?"

"Why, at the palace..."

"It's true then!" she shrieked. Several people passing by hurried away in fear of the disembodied voice. "Court her all you want, you'll never have her!"

To a god, it all happened so slowly: the way she drew the butcher knife out from under her cloak, the way she thrust it into his stomach, the way his eyes bulged when he realized what she'd done, the way his own gore stained his hands. So slowly, I should have been able to intercede, but performed with such hatred I was literally repulsed. I am not Apollo; I do not have the gift to undo what she did.

I curse myself for being as blind as men say I am. I've seen passionate women slip from love to hatred and back before. I should have known this might happen to Francesca and found a way to help her keep her love true. But most of all, I'm furious I didn't understand the nature of Elisabeth's curse sooner. She hadn't just cursed her family and the Montagues; she had cursed love's ability to unite enemies. A love between a Montague and a Capulet will never last; it will always change to hate. Never before had such a strong curse been directed against me, but I have a plan to counter it.

Dearest, please beg of Pluto a pair of jars enchanted to stay as cold as His realm. Have Mercury leave them at the fountain I told you about. Tell both of them to hurry. Time moves more swiftly in the human world than it does for gods, and if I miss the moment, we will be forever doomed.

Missing you,

Cupid

Dearest Psyche,

How weary I grow of the human world! Such constant motion and change batters my eternal nature. How I long for our home on Olympus, far from human eyes. I cannot rest until we embrace. Only your letters help me endure this exile.

You must wonder if we will ever see each other again. Given how the houses of Montague and Capulet dwindle, I worry their lines will die out before the curse. The current Montague married late, and his wife has been barren for several years. But today she bore a son named Romeo. This couple is now a family, and I see them caring for their child with devotion that surpasses their love for each other. Strange how family love is so strong even without divine intervention. I always thought the romantic love I create is the most powerful type of love, but now I'm not so sure.

I celebrated Romeo's birth by catching his first breath in one of the jars you obtained for me. Nothing can be more innocent than a child's first breath, and innocence is the ally of pure love. Romeo's breath turned to liquid as it entered the jar. I sealed the lid with beeswax and hid the jar for safety.

Romeo provided me with only half a kiss; now I need the first breath of a Capulet maiden. Unfortunately, Capulet's wife has already lost several children before they were born. Plead with Juno for me, Dearest. Sweeten her temper with honeycakes and mead until she agrees to send a girl to the Capulets.

Love and kisses,

Cupid

Dearest Psyche,

Praise Juno and all the others of our pantheon! A daughter has been born to the Capulet family, and her parents couldn't be happier. Her name is Juliet, and I have captured her first breath as I did Romeo Montague's.

The Montagues have had no more children, and though Juliet's mother survived the birth, I fear she will never bear another child. There is another Capulet child, a male named Tybalt, but even if he were a suitable match for Romeo—my divine arrows cannot make two men love each other unless they have that inclination—Tybalt is too far removed from the main Capulet line to break the curse.

So, Romeo and Juliet are our last chance, Darling. It will not be much longer; the newborn girl will be old enough for marriage in an eyeblink. Don't worry about making sure the house is clean for my return; all I want to see is you.

Passionately,

Cupid

Dearest Psyche,

At long last, Romeo and Juliet have met!

I've had a hard time keeping Romeo's heart free, as he is eager to give it away. Whenever he fancied himself in love with a lady, I shot a blunt arrow of lead through her heart. She soon turned from him, leaving him to pine until his friends distracted him.

Juliet is scarcely fourteen, but her family is planning her marriage. They prepared a feast honoring Paris, a relation of the prince. They hoped I'd shoot arrows of love through Paris's and Juliet's hearts, but I had other plans.

Lord Capulet foolishly gave a list of guests to an illiterate servant, so I guided the servant to Romeo. I'd recently caused his latest beloved, Rosalind, to prefer chastity over him, and he was wailing for her in his usual fashion. But once his friends learned of Capulet's masque, they convinced him to attend it with them.

Now it was time for me to use the breaths I had saved, and I had only a few mortal hours to do it.

I hurried back to where I'd hidden the jars. I scraped off the beeswax, pried off the lids, and looked inside. Had I been human, my heart would have skipped a beat, for at first I thought the breaths had escaped. Then I saw the faintest frost lining the jar and realized the breaths had frozen. Only something warmer than the Underworld to thaw them. I'd have to use my own divine blood.

I unpacked my quiver until I came to my most potent arrow, the one of gold and diamond. This one had been made by Vulcan himself and could pierce any heart, mortal or divine. This arrow made me fall in love with you, Dearest. It can't pierce my heart again while our love still lives, but I still deemed it safest to apply the tip to my wrist.

I felt no pain at first. In fact, it felt quite pleasant, like the vanilla-honey taste of ambrosia or the glorious sound of the Muses in song. But then the arrow bit deeper. I felt as my own the pain of lovers separated by circumstances they couldn't control, the disappointment and sense of betrayal when the beloved turned out not to be as lovely or as charming as he or she first seemed, the times lovers felt angry enough with each other to quarrel....

I remembered too the night you woke me with burning candle wax, and how I had to leave the idyllic retreat that had become more of a home to me than Mount Olympus.

I cried out, and the first drop of my blood beaded slowly, clinging to my flesh before falling into Romeo's jar. Steam rose up; I had to cover the jar before his breath could escape.

The wound was already starting to close; I inserted the arrowhead in it before it could completely heal. I fumbled the lid partway off of Juliet's jar, then held my wrist in position and pushed the arrow in deeper.

The second time was worse. I experienced now what it was like to be married to an unloving, unfaithful wife. (Thank Jupiter you're not like that!) I watched through a wife's eyes as her beloved husband became a shadow of himself as he ceaselessly drank, becoming more and more bad-tempered. And I felt grief in my own heart with all the spouses who'd stood by the graveside of their other halves. The shock, the anger, the numbness that made life unbearable, just like the anguish I feel now.

The second drop rolled into Juliet's jar. I covered it and dropped my golden arrow on the floor.

Psyche, I'd thought you'd taught me more about love than even this god knew. But there are more facets to the joys and sorrows of love than there are drops of water in the ocean. Even though I focus on physical love, lust creates children and families and so many other things mortals care about. It is something to think about later.

I materialized in Capulet's main hall as Romeo and his friends arrived. Taking on a servant's appearance, I picked up a tray of wine goblets, clearing it of all but one, and poured Romeo's and Juliet's breaths into it. They swirled into a kiss. Then I presented the goblet to Romeo, watching as he drank the spiced wine and kiss in a single swallow. His downcast face regained its glow, and he glanced at Juliet, dancing with Paris at her parents' request.

"What lady enriches the hand of yonder knight?" Romeo asked me.

I pretended ignorance. "I know not, sir."

"She teaches the torches how to burn bright!" As he waxed eloquent, I backed away so I could disappear.

As soon as the dance ended, Romeo joined the next one, waiting until he was partnered with Juliet. He exchanged pretty words with her as I flew overhead and grabbed an arrow.

"Thus sin from my lips is purged by yours," Romeo said. He leaned forward and touched her lips with his, allowing her to taste the special kiss I'd made for them. She drew back, but it was too late; love flushed her cheeks.

"Then my lips have taken your sin," she managed to say.

"'Sin from my lips! O trespass sweetly urged! Give me my sin again.'"

Romeo pulled her closer for a longer kiss. While they were pressed together, I aimed carefully and shot both their hearts with a single arrow.

Juliet's face was completely red by the time Romeo let her go. She had trouble breathing for several moments. Finally, trying in vain to bring herself under control, she said in a severe tone, "'You kiss by the book.'" Her eyes said otherwise.

So it is done, Dearest. He returned to her house later that night to woo her, and she agreed to wed him the next day. Look for me soon after this letter arrives—or perhaps I shall overtake it in my haste to return to you.

Impatiently,

Cupid

Dearest, long-suffering Psyche,

Oh, woe! Has any god ever borne such pain as we have known? No sooner was Romeo wed than he was banished from Verona for killing his secret wife's cousin, Tybalt. Thankfully, the kiss I'd created for him and Juliet preserved her love for him even through this crisis. But an unsought marriage of Juliet to another threatened permanent separation of the lovers.

Do you think I didn't try to help them? I was there, whispering ideas into the priest's head—vowing chastity for the crucified god did not make him immune to lust—to help him smuggle Juliet, feigning death, out of the city. But the priest's message to Romeo went undelivered, and he despaired. He poisoned himself in her tomb minutes before she woke. To my horror, she stabbed herself, and the lines of both the Capulets and the Montagues ended in blood.

Elisabeth's ring tightened on my finger, and her spirit cackled in triumph. "See, God of Supposed Love? They may have killed themselves instead of each other, but they're still dead. You'll stay on Earth forever, fooling others that love is divine when it's a curse from demons."

For a moment I imagined a future separated from you and our daughter. I remembered the pain I'd felt when I shed my own blood, but I also remembered the love Romeo and Juliet's parents have for their children. If romantic love was impossible now, another type of love might still unite them.

There was divine blood in both Romeo and Juliet, not just what they'd inherited from Jupiter, but the drops I'd shed to form their first kiss. Gore from Romeo's battle with Paris still smeared his doublet.

I pulled out my gold-and-diamond arrow. Remembering you gave me the strength to shed a tear, cleaning the tip and passing on my grief. I dipped the arrowhead in Juliet's blood, then Romeo's. I hadn't been able to collect their last breaths, but I pressed the arrow against their cooling lips anyway. Then I drew my bow and waited.

The commotion at the tomb drew the prince of the city and the leading families out to investigate. Juliet's father arrived soon after the prince. I took aim, not to inspire lust, but empathy for another man who'd also lost his only beloved child. My arrow circled around at my silent command, ready for me to shoot again when Romeo's father appeared. His hand was already on his sword when I shot him, but as the other mortals at the scene pieced together what had happened, his aggression faded. At the end, Capulet and Montague embraced, united in grief.

I whispered to Elisabeth's ring, "Poor Juliet and Romeo may have lost their chance to live and love, but their sacrifices have freed their fathers from hate. And listen how they promise to keep the memory of their children alive. Their love will be celebrated forever. This family love will last, Elisabeth. And your curse—will not."

Her ring slipped off my finger, whining as it fell. To make sure the curse was dead, I scratched the ring with my diamond arrow.

This time I'm truly coming home, Psyche. Send everyone away so we can celebrate our reunion in private. But when we are finally sated, let us have our daughter, my mother, and your sisters—yes, bring them back from the Underworld!—visit us. Perhaps once they hear this tale, they will learn families should never drive lovers apart, and that families depend on lovers to survive.

Your husband forevermore,

Cupid

The Owl and the Spider's Son

I feel no remorse for Arachne's fall. She woke me and my nestlings with her proud boasts. As soon as I heard the name of my beloved mistress, Athena, I knew I had to learn what the mortals were saying about her, sun or no sun.

My mate was sleeping close by in another tree, so I knew he would protect our children if there was any trouble. Keeping to the shadows as much as possible, I glided to a nearby stream. A dozen naiads poked their heads out of the water and admired a tapestry held aloft by a young woman. Her cloak shimmered like water, and a gold wreath crowned her dark hair. Was she beautiful? I don't know how humans judge such things. She held herself as proudly as if she were a goddess, or a predator searching for prey among her own kind.

"Surely Athena herself must have blessed you, Arachne," the naiad closest to the human woman said. She reached for the tapestry, but the human moved before water could drop onto it.

"I need no blessing from Athena, or any other god," the woman declared. "I'm a better weaver than her."

As the naiads gasped and dove into their stream, I was able to see the tapestry Arachne had woven. It depicted a stag being torn apart by hounds. Blood ran from the hounds' teeth as if they devoured real flesh, not dyed cloth. I stared, fascinated, at the prey many times larger than me. It took me several moments to realize the stag's face seemed to shift into an agonized human's every time Arachne waved the cloth. In the background, naked, hungry-looking women caressed each other while staring at the slaughter. The one in the center held a silver bow that could only belong to Artemis.

This woman, this Arachne, might be almost as skilled as my mistress, but she had no respect for any of the goddesses. Athena would want to know of this right away. Despite the harsh sunlight and the taunts of crows, I flew up to Mount Olympus and shared what I had learned with the great, the immortal Athena, weaving her own tribute to her glorious father. She frowned, and a thread snarled in her hand.

"Show me this mortal," Athena said. "If she doesn't learn some humility, she'll learn a lesson no human will ever forget."

* * *

Humans who understand the art of weaving--and can appreciate color--have written about the contest between my mistress and the arrogant mortal. They've described how Athena disguised herself as an old woman and visited Arachne--though no one mentioned the owl perched on the roof, listening to her mistress chiding the woman for her impiety. Such was the mercy of my goddess; she would have forgiven Arachne if she'd repented and shown gratitude for her gifts. Instead, the woman made it worse for herself. I almost tumbled over when I heard Arachne say, "I don't believe in the gods, crone; they're stories meant to scare us into behaving a certain way. And if they do exist, they can't possibly be as powerful or skillful as they claim. I've never met anyone who could weave expression into faces the way I do. Why, if Athena were here right now, I'd show her who the best weaver in the world is."

The silence was so complete even my sensitive hearing couldn't pick up a breath from a mouse. I hunkered down, wishing I was safe in my hollow tree. Athena's wrath is terrible, but when she serves her anger death-cold, there's no flying from her.

"You should be careful what you wish for, child," Athena said. Light flashed from below, and I felt myself summoned. I flew through an open window to perch on her shoulder. She'd abandoned her disguise and showed herself tall and graceful, clad in purest white. Athena stared at her with wide eyes in a pale face, but she didn't cower. She was nothing more than a mouse foolish enough to think itself as fierce as an owl.

"If it's a contest you want, a contest we shall have." Athena gestured, and her loom appeared, securing itself next to Arachne's. Weights and baskets overflowing with prepared wool threatened to topple onto a cradle. I hooted softly, and the goddess cleared a space around the infant. "We shall weave for three days and three nights. Then we will see who the best weaver in the world is!"

Blood returned to Arachne's face. "We shall indeed," she said, with a faint smirk suggesting she already thought herself the winner.

Woman and goddess stood in front of their looms, selected colors, and went to work.

Time passed oddly for me during their contest, as if my mistress had me wrapped in her spell. I neither hungered nor felt thirst; my talons remained locked in place on Athena's cloak. I remember periods of light and dark, of other people crowding into the tiny house but never coming within arm's length of us. Every now and then in the background, I heard a child's thin wail, quickly hushed. It made me uneasy, as if there was something else I was supposed to be doing, but I was woven into this contest as if the wool threads strapped my wings down. Athena's fingers danced between the warp strings. As she completed each row, the cloth folded itself up. Yet despite the inherent disadvantage of her humanity, Arachne kept pace with my mistress.

Athena and Arachne stepped away from their looms at the same instant. Athena ordered the tapestries cut down and brought into the closest temple so they could be unrolled and displayed. Even an eagle would have been hard-pressed to find a flaw in either tapestry. Athena's offering was suitable for such a holy place; each of the gods and goddesses of Mount Olympus looked regal on their thrones. Athena illustrated herself giving an olive tree to the city of Athens. Arachne's work, on the other hand, insulted the deities. Zeus, Athena's beloved father, fared the worst, as Arachne depicted every instance he'd transformed himself into a beast--sadly, not an owl--to seduce a human woman.

"You insolent harlot!" Athena rent the blasphemous work in two. For the first time, Arachne cowered, but it was too late to appease my mistress.

"Go, my messenger." She launched me off of her shoulder. "Fly to Hecate and bring me the potion in the bottle with eight rubies."

I traveled to the nearest crossroads. Hecate rose from the ground and handed me the bottle Athena had requested. I meant to fly back with it straightaway, but I heard another owl hooting mournfully nearby. With a shock, I realized it was my mate. I hurried to him, the bottle weighing me down with every stroke of my wings.

I didn't even make it to the nest before my mate screeched at me. "Where have you been? I had to hunt for the brood all by myself, with no one to guard the nestlings. They were all taken!"

Stunned, I checked out the cavity myself. It was true; only down feathers remained. Our nestlings were too young to have fledged successfully. This was the third brood my mate and I had raised together. We've had eggs that never hatched and tiny nestlings that didn't thrive, but we've never had a failure like this before. I reached out to groom my mate, but he pecked at me.

Heavy-hearted, I continued my mission. Surely by next winter my mate would forgive me, and we would do better with our next brood. In the meantime, my mistress still needed me.

The temple was empty, so I sought Athena at Arachne's house. It looked like the site of a crazed hunt. Arachne's tapestry hung in shreds, and skeins of yarn had uncoiled among what was left of the broken furniture. It didn't surprise me that my warrior mistress had demolished the place, but even I was taken aback to find Arachne hanging from the highest beam in her house, suspended by blood-red wool.

"She hung herself out of damaged pride when I refused to admit her blasphemous work was flawless," Athena said. "But there's still breath in her. Quick, give me the potion." Athena smiled grimly as she poured it over Arachne. "I'll make sure she continues to spin and weave till the end of her days, she and her—"

Instinct told me she planned to curse this woman's unfortunate descendants. The nurse poked her head inside the house, as if she was here to give the child to its doom. Hadn't enough younglings suffered already?

I positioned myself between Athena and the baby. Spreading my wings to their full span, I cried, "Great Athena, for my sake, grant mercy to one child today. My brood are gone, but why should this nestling suffer?"

Some of the anger faded from Athena's gray eyes. "Your brood, faithful owl?"

I told her briefly how my children had perished during the contest.

A goddess as great as Athena never apologizes, especially not to a mere animal. But though she remains eternally virgin, she is wise enough to understand a mother's pain. She stroked my head lightly with a finger. "Have hope, my servant. You may be a mother again before the season turns. For your sake, I will spare the son." She gestured toward the nurse, who bowed as low as she could. "He will contribute to weaving in his own way. But the daughters of Arachne will share her fate, lest they share her hubris."

Now I saw for myself the effect of Hecate's potion. Arachne had shrunk until she was small enough to snatch in my beak. Her body had become hard and round, with eight limbs sticking out of it. As she scrambled up the wall, a thread of silk followed her.

* * *

The rest turned out as Athena predicted. She never again summoned me during nesting season. As I raised brood after brood, I watched Arachne's son, Closter, grow to manhood and invent the spindle. Arachne's daughters multiplied, spinning their webs. Every time I spy one, I inspect it for any hints of outrage against the gods.

Rather than trouble Athena again, I will eat the offender myself.

Silver Rain

I'm the only one in this town who hates the silver rain.

Every spring, there's a stretch of a week or ten days where the rain comes down silver with illusion. It doesn't just wash our town; it transforms it. Cottages become palaces, twigs turn into giant oaks, and crows look like peacocks. Only people are untouched. Travelers come from miles around, even from other countries, to experience it. My bakery makes more that week than it does any other month of the year.

A pity I can't enjoy the visions of the silver rain. To me, the town seems to be the same whether it rains or not. My father could never tell red from green, but other than needing us to help him match his clothes, his color blindness didn't affect his life. I have to keep my mouth shut when tourists come in, exclaiming about the illusions and congratulating me on my good fortune to see the silver rain every year.

The silver rain brought me love, then washed it away.

* * *

His name was Tam, a poet who'd wandered into our town from far away seeking the inspiration of the rain. His hair was dark like ink, and his eyes green as the new leaves of spring.

I may be too practical for magic, but he taught me a line or two of poetry. And why not? You may not believe me now, when all you see is a stooped old woman with rotten teeth and hair too gray and stringy to be compared to the silver rain. But in my youth, I was considered fair. I stood straight and tall, my hair shone golden in the sun, and my eyes were deep blue, not watered down by time and tears.

He strolled into my father's bakery, seeking a roll or fresh loaf of bread. All he had to pay with was a song, and that was coin too light, too fleeting, for my father to accept in his till. Then the stranger smiled at me, showing teeth as straight as the trees. A faint drizzle clung to his cheeks. His skin was lightly tanned, his shoulders and chest broad. I saw in his warm smile and bright eyes his pleasure at seeing a seventeen-year-old woman who'd just come into her beauty.

Seeing myself so reflected in his eyes, how could I not help but fall in love with him?

To me, a smile like that was well worth a roll or three, and I passed them to the young man when my father turned away to scold Peter, my younger brother, for letting the bread burn. Then a flock of gossips poured into the bakery, eyeing the stranger as if he were an iced bun ready to pop in their mouths. By the time I was done waiting on them— this meant letting them thump every loaf in the store twice—my stranger was gone, leaving me with nothing but a sigh and an aching heart.

I didn't expect to see him again, but at twilight when we closed, he was waiting by the door. He graced me with another smile that warmed me to my toes. "Thank you for the rolls earlier."

This close to him, I could smell the scents of pine and musk, not the sweat and grease and onions of the local youths. "Who are you?"

He bowed his head. "I'm Tam, my lady."

I blushed; no one ever called a baker's daughter a lady. And Tam, such an exotic name.

"And what's your name?" he prodded.

What would he think of it? "Marthe."

"A lovely name."

It wasn't; it was an ugly name, as solid as my grandmother, who had borne it first.

He studied me for a moment before saying, "But perhaps you will let me give you a new name, a special one for the silver rain. What would you like?"

Such an idea was so strange to me I had no idea what to suggest.

"May I pick one for you?" he asked.

"Can you do that?"

He grinned and held his head high, displaying his sharp jaw and straight nose. "I'm a poet, a weaver of words and wonder. I shall name you..." he deepened his voice, "Lilla!"

I tried the name on, rolling it around my tongue. Lilla for a flower, something unworldly and delicate. I'd never pictured myself that way, but suddenly I wanted it more than anything.

"Do you like it?"

I nodded, and he drew closer. I wanted to touch his mouth, share his gift for words. If I couldn't see the illusions myself, I could hear them in his voice, and I longed to experience them for myself.

Before we could kiss, my father shouted, "Marthe! Where are you?"

I jumped. Heat flooded my face, even though I'd done nothing wrong. "Father?"

"What are you doing standing about? Your mother needs your help!"

By the time I turned to say farewell to Tam, he was gone. A silver raindrop kissed my cheek, but all it felt like was cold and wet, not wondrous.

* * *

When I woke up the next morning, the silver rain had begun in earnest. It sheeted over the buildings and streets as if a poor but proud lady meant to cover her mended and tattered furnishings before guests came. She had succeeded; strangers draped in oiled cloaks gasped, pointed, and laughed, their faces as open as children's. Even my father on his way to the shop looked around, smiling. But he didn't bother describing what he saw to me. I kept my gaze on the foul-smelling puddles mixed with mud and dung. Funny how no one else seemed to mind them this time of year.

I tried to keep the resentment out of my voice and face as I waited on customers. I didn't quite succeed, but our shop was so full Father had no time to scold me. Peter was less lucky, but since he got up in the middle of the night to tend the dough and the ovens, he was able to escape in the middle of the afternoon.

I didn't leave the shop until almost sunset. I didn't get far before someone grabbed me from behind. Fortunately, I recognized Tam's scent, or else I would have kicked his shin.

"Come with me, Lilla," he murmured into my ear. "Come see what the silver rain has done to your town."

If only I could. Even if my family didn't need me, I couldn't see the wonders everyone else did. I opened my mouth to tell him of my blindness to magic when Katherin walked by.

Katherin had been born during the silver rain, and she acted as if she had suckled it in with her mother's milk. Was she really prettier than all the other girls, as the young men claimed? She appeared shrewish to me. Over the years, she'd wheedled scraps of colored fabric and cracked glass beads from vendors at the summer fair, and she'd crafted them into an outfit, that made her look as rich as a queen. The mud dared not stain her bare feet, and her head was tipped high, allowing her fake crown to glisten against her red coils. She wore her costume every year during the silver rain, hoping to seduce some visiting noble into marriage. She'd already received one proposal, one that I'd inadvertently ruined later by blurting out how poor she was within earshot of her fiancé. Since then, she'd played tricks on me at every turn.

Tam's gaze followed her, and his lips moved. Had he adopted a new muse? Before I realized what I was doing, I clamped my hands over his before he could let me go. My hips bumped his. "I'll be glad to go with you."

Katherin's hot stare burned through my back as we left, but I didn't care about that. Her laugh was disturbing, however.

Tam led me to the village square where the fair and other festivals were held. It was already crammed with masked visitors too busy gawking to move aside. Off to the side, someone fiddled a lively tune, and the smell of roast chestnuts reminded me how long it had been since breakfast.

Tam jumped onto a wagon off to the side, then pulled me up next to him. "Look there!" He gestured at the clock tower. "I've never seen such a shining castle. Have you?"

How could I answer? "No, never." That was true enough.

"Are these visions the same from year to year?"

I shook my head. I'd gleamed that much through overheard conversations.

Tam turned his attention to another part of the market, the archway over the main road in and out of town. "The bridge...the gold gleams like the sun come to Earth. And down below, the fairies dance in mirth."

He went on, improvising rhymes about gem-studded walls, mythical animals, and buildings designed into fantastic shapes. As I listened, I fancied I could see the things he described, wavering in and out of existence around the ordinary objects graced by the silver rain. Was this what everyone else saw, or did they see it more clearly? It must have been more real for others, or else why would they be so enraptured over such fragile illusions? Yet this was more than I'd ever seen in my life. I wanted to weep, I wanted to run over and touch them, I wanted to demand more all at once. What I did instead was cling to Tam's hand as if he could grant me deeper visions.

Every now and then someone broke their gaze from the surroundings to stare at us. Were they wondering how a baker's daughter came to be with such a fine man? The thought thrilled me almost as much as Tam's words.

He didn't run out of words until the moon had risen, though that was more due to his voice growing hoarse than lack of creativity on his part. When a fit of coughing seized him, I gently led him down from the wagon. "Which inn are you staying at?" I asked him.

He shivered. "The Swan and Bull."

That was one of the cheaper inns, known more for their beer and serving women than their food or clean beds. Father would be displeased if he ever learned I'd been there. But I wasn't sure Tam could make it that far without my help, so I draped my sodden shawl over my head and let him lean on me as we staggered to the inn. By the time we arrived, Tam couldn't speak for coughing. I promised the innkeep whatever bread I could scavenge tomorrow for as much hot soup as Tam could swallow.

"Thank you, Lilla," he said absently. Even his kiss, though pressed on my waiting lips, seemed elsewhere, remembering perhaps Katherin's beauty—or the silver rain.

As I hurried home, I hoped the silver rain would last this year. What if Tam left with the rain? I couldn't abandon my family, not even if he asked me to. If I lost him, I'd never see beauty again.

* * *

The days blurred as if the rain washed them together: endless hours of serving in my father's bakery, enlivened only by my evenings with Tam. We'd sit side-by-side in a beer garden as he read to me the lines he'd composed while I'd worked. Then we'd dance, twirling faster when drunks shouted insults at us. Or we'd walk, and Tam's words would turn any alley into the main street of a fairy town.

After that first night, I made sure to bring my warmest scarves with me in the morning so I could drape them about his neck when he met me at sunset. I brought out my few coins to buy us hot spiced wine to soothe his throat. And after one particularly fine night when he wove me into his poetry, I helped to warm his bed afterward, dashing home once he'd fallen asleep, grinning despite my soreness.

My mother shook me awake the next morning, saying, "Get up, lazy one! You can rest when the rain is over." Overhead, the perpetual hammering of rain on our roof had slowed. Within the next day or two, the silver rain would end, taking with it the enchantment it had cast over our town—and my poet with them.

The bakery was already slower than before, giving me too much time to fret. Would Tam consider staying in my town once the silver rain ended for the year? My parents were hinting I should accept one of the local's proposals and bring someone else into the bakery. Even if Tam returned next year, I might not be free, or he might not remember me. But the thought of leaving this town, the only home I'd ever known, frightened me as well.

Katherin flounced into the bakery late in the day to pick up fresh-baked loaves for dinner, announcing to all who cared—or didn't—that her family was hosting some of the richer visitors tonight. "I think their son might ask for my hand," she said, tossing her hair. "Of course, not all of us will get a wedding out of the silver rain, right, Marthe? Some of us find toads instead."

I couldn't resist. "Like your intended?"

Her eyes narrowed, and I couldn't help but feel a small spike of satisfaction.

She approached my counter until we were face-to-face. "I know you can't see the silver rain illusions," she said, "but I didn't know you were blind to male beauty too."

"My poet is far finer than any of the other men in this town!"

"A poet? Is that what you see in him?" Her complexion developed blotches as I watched. "Are you deaf too? Why would a poet take up with the one woman in town who can't appreciate his art?"

"That's not true! I've listened to every word of his and committed it to heart."

She smirked with a grin that would have flattened a thousand loaves. "But you can't see what he describes."

I shook my head. "His words make the silver rain come alive for me."

"Does he know that?"

I took too long before saying, "He doesn't need to."

Her face aged to a hag's. "Then what would you give me—"

I recoiled from her sagging skin and rheumy eyes.

"What's wrong?" Her face returned to normal, but I still couldn't get over the shock.

She touched her cheeks and chin. "What's wrong? Tell me."

"You...you're as ugly outside as you are inside."

She shrieked and ran out of the store without her bread.

"Marthe! What happened?" My father asked.

"I don't know." What had happened? Was it a trick of light, lack of sleep, or something else?

What did she mean by Tam being ugly? She must have been trying to upset me; it fit her character. Tam was pure and good. If the silver rain affected people, he would have appeared to be an angel.

Whenever I fretted, I cleaned. That afternoon, I didn't allow muddy footprints to remain on the floor for longer than it took my father to shape a loaf of bread.

* * *

I looked for Tam as soon as I left the shop that evening, but he wasn't waiting by the door as he always did. I hurried to the square, which was already less crowded with visitors. That should have made it easier to pick him out, but he wasn't there. I searched several other popular vistas—the city walls, the garden by the mayor's house, and the church—without success. Finally I returned to the Swan and Bull. Perhaps he'd had a relapse of the coughing fit.

When I entered the inn, I immediately spotted him, as handsome as ever, alone in a booth with several empty tankards beside him. At least Katherin wasn't with him. But when I approached Tam, I could tell she'd already been there. Why else would he look at me with such disappointment?

"My beautiful Lilla is really a Marthe after all," he murmured.

My chest ached, as if he'd taken out my heart when he withdrew the beautiful name he'd given me. "But...but, when I was with you, I really was Lilla." I reached for his hand, but it drifted away as if of its own power.

"Why didn't you tell me you couldn't see the effects of the silver rain?" he asked me.

Because I knew he'd react like this, but you can't tell a man something like that. Besides, it wasn't completely true anymore. I sat down across from him and looked directly into his eyes. "When I heard your poetry, I could almost see the castles and the fairy lights and everything."

His eyes lit up, though the rest of his expression didn't change. "Is that true?"

"It is."

"Lilla...that's the greatest gift you could have given me! Every poet wants to know his words have an effect on others." Smiling now, he rose, then pulled me out of my seat and swept me into a brief dance. I thrilled to his touch, his scent. He murmured in my ear, "If this is the last night of the silver rain, let's make the most of it. I'll show you the wonders of your town, and later you can show me your personal wonders."

I giggled, as he'd probably meant to make me do, and we proceeded to follow his plan. But later, while we lay in each other's arms, I couldn't help but sigh.

Tam traced a lazy curve over my breasts. "What's wrong, Lilla?"

"What happens after tomorrow, Tam?"

He was silent for a moment before replying. "I have to return to my patron. He expects me to deliver my verses and recite them myself, in front of an audience."

"How far do you have to travel?" Would he be able to return?

"Very far. It'll take me more than a month."

I wanted to weep but didn't. "Will I ever see you again?"

"I don't know. It depends on my patron. He may let me travel on my own again, or he may insist I remain by his side. No matter what, I'll think of you fondly." He fingered a gold chain around his neck. "Would you like something to remember me by?"

I would, even though I feared my parents' wrath if they found it. I would have to hide it under my dress.

After he draped the necklace in place, we kissed each other, memorizing each other's taste. Feeling greatly daring, I slipped my tongue into his mouth. I wanted not just his taste, but the feel of those perfect, even teeth—

Which were crooked.

I jerked back. Where was my Tam? This stranger wasn't handsome. He was balding, with pockmarked skin, bushy eyebrows, and a thick nose. He wasn't as tall as Tam either, closer to my length. Only his eyes were Tam's, green and clear.

We stared at each other, the silence deeper than before. Even the faint tinkling of rain on the window had vanished.

"Who are you?" I asked.

"I'm still Tam." The cadence was still the same, but his voice had shifted slightly in some way I couldn't pinpoint. "Why? What's wrong?"

"You look completely different."

He raised his eyebrows. "I do?"

"You were handsome before, but now you're not!" I remembered the stares, the catcalls others had hurled our way. Was this the man everyone else had seen? The heat from my face could have browned a rack of loaves. Katherin and everyone else would never let me forget what a fool I'd made of myself.

"It's true what your friend said before, that you can't see the illusions the silver rain cast over your town?"

I nodded.

He cupped my chin, forcing me to look at him. "Perhaps, my Lilla, you see something even rarer. Perhaps for you, the silver rain works on people."

"Or perhaps you glamoured me." I cast the blanket aside, left the bed, and gathered my clothes. Cold stole some of my heat, but not enough to ease my embarrassment and anger.

"Me? The only magic I have is my poetry."

I wished that was all the magic at work here. Without saying anything else, I left.

I was already home before I remembered Katherin's face and how it had switched between young and old. Many of the people I'd noticed during the silver rain had appeared to be wearing masks, but I hadn't seen any for sale. Maybe Tam had been right after all; maybe the rain did affect how I saw other people. How come it had never happened before? Womanhood had come late to me; only in the last year had I started my courses. Could that be a factor? I owed Tam an apology and a better farewell. It didn't matter what he looked like; I loved him and would follow him to his patron if he would take me. I resolved to rise with my brother so I could join Tam before he left town.

I slept poorly, so I knew when Peter left the house. Still yawning, I followed him. I reached Tam's inn well before dawn, but when I climbed up to his room, it was already empty of him and his bag of possessions.

I raced back down to the stable, where one of the grooms snored as he slept. I shook him awake. "Quick, man! Did anyone leave in the night?"

He stared at me as if I were daft, then shook his head.

I roused every worker I could find at the inn, but none of them had seen Tam, even when I described his true appearance. Finally the innkeep's wife came downstairs, covering her yawn with a scrap of paper.

"You must be Marthe."

I flinched at the use of my real name.

She continued, "This was shoved under my door. Take it and leave my staff alone."

The paper had been folded over, with my now-hated first name on the outside. Inside, it read, "She who loves the face, not the heart, Forever from me must soon part."

I crumpled the note so tightly in my fist I had difficulty unclenching it when I arrived at the bakery. I threw the note onto the fire and right away wished I hadn't. But it was too late to retrieve it.

* * *

Katherin married her nobleman during the next silver rain, in the town square. Everyone agreed it was a beautiful setting for a beautiful bride. Everyone, that is, except me. I saw a wolf's head in place of her own.

The more I looked, the more I saw how others' faces changed in the rain. Those who were good became comely; the ugly of heart became ugly in truth. Some, who were exactly what they seemed, never changed.

I wondered what my own face looked like, but I never checked, no matter how many puddles tempted me.

As for me, I never married. My nights with Tam had ruined me for the good and unchanging, and I refused the bad. Tam didn't even leave me with a child. I've had plenty of free time to build up my father's bakery before selling it for a nice profit.

Now I spend my days dunking bread into ale and trying to find and read poetry books. Sometimes I think I recognize a line or verse as his, but it always belongs to someone else. I keep looking, though. When I find his poetry, I will memorize it and recite it in the middle of the silver rain. If I'm lucky, I'll glimpse castles again instead of altered faces. Maybe then Tam will return to me—or even a stranger wearing his features.

Either way, this time I want the illusion to last.

Bugged Out at the Museum

It was Dr. William Meadows' least favorite weekend of the year, Members' Night weekend. He didn't mind the late hours—his best writing hours were around midnight—but he detested the intrusion into his privacy. The rest of the year, he could count on the third level of the museum to be quiet, the wooden beams high overhead giving the hall a measure of dignity. Now instead they rang with the constant footsteps of visitors. And children. Lots of children, running and poking their snotty noses into properly organized displays. Even though no food was allowed up here, William was sure the children's hands were still sticky from spilled drinks. Every time a kid picked up his favorite specimen— a Goliath beetle that he'd nicknamed Golly—he flinched, certain that one of the legs would come off. If his boss hadn't ordered him to stand here, smile, and answer questions, he'd be locked in his office until Monday.

Only half an hour, and this level is closed. William glanced at his smartphone, urging the numbers to turn over more rapidly. Out of the corner of his eye, he saw a family approach. Father, mother pushing a cranky toddler in a stroller, and a young boy, between five and seven, touching everything despite admonitions from his father to leave them alone. Even the stuffed animal he clutched seemed to knock something over whenever the boy stepped up to a table. William covered Golly with some extra flyers before the boy could grab him.

The boy stopped in front of William's table and stared at his collection, with all the specimens neatly labeled. His eyes grew as round as a ladybug's spots. "That's a lot of bugs!" he said in a high-pitched voice that grated William's eardrums. "I've never seen so many bugs before!"

"There are plenty more downstairs, in the cases."

The child failed to get the hint. He pawed at another beetle, a small one. "I like to watch bugs in my yard," he continued. "I like to watch ants. They fight a lot."

William remembered his own childhood. He'd always been shorter than his classmates, so he preferred to hide in his own backyard or somewhere remote where no one could find him and study nature for hours. That had led to his eventual majoring in biology, his Ph.D., and his decades spent at this museum caring for its insect collection. He supposed he should thank his childhood bullies for steering him onto this path, but they didn't deserve thanks. People had always been cruel to him; that's why he preferred bugs.

"Do you have any bugs here that would be good for fighting?" the boy asked. The tail of his stuffed lion flicked the papers off of Golly. Immediately the boy's eyes lit up. "Hey, that's a good one!"

"Please don't touch it," William said. "It's delicate." His hand automatically moved to block the boy, but William hesitated, fearing the contact. Before William could transfer Golly somewhere safer, the boy touched it first.

For an instant, the air around the beetle glowed as if a light was concealed under the shell. Then Golly's legs jerked, and he twitched, opening his first pair of protective wings to expose the second. William simply stared. How was this possible? Golly had been part of the museum collection longer than this child had existed. He couldn't be alive after all this time. Maybe William was imagining the movement.

As if to prove he was alive, Golly sank his mandibles into the stuffed lion's tail. The genial expression stitched on its face changed to one of shock. Then, with a tiny roar, the lion whirled and batted Golly with a paw. William winced, but Golly appeared unhurt. The beetle swiped at the animated tiger with his tarsi—what laymen called claws—and drew stuffing out of its belly.

With a wail, the boy snatched his lion away from Golly and cradled it to his chest. "Mom, Roary got hurt! That bad bug did it!"

The child reached for Golly again, but this time he hesitated. William didn't; handling insects was routine to him. Golly climbed into his hand, fitting into his palm perfectly. William slipped his hand behind the case, where Golly would be safe from the boy. A terrible thought gripped William; what if the boy could take away his magic and leave Golly dead again? A foolish notion, considering Golly had been dead for years, but William didn't want to see his longtime companion lose the new life he'd been given.

The boy turned to his mother and showed her his lion's injury. She shrugged. "Accidents happen, honey. You have to be more careful with Roary. I won't be able to sew him back together until we get home."

"But look!" The child pointed to the fluff spilling out of the tear. "He needs help now." His lip trembled.

I guess that toy means a lot to him, like it's his favorite friend. William reached for Golly, who nuzzled his finger. Maybe this boy was more like William than he'd realized. If so, then perhaps he could—had to—help.

"I have some tape in my office," he said. "Maybe even some bandages. They'll hold your toy—your lion—together until your mom can fix it. Is that OK?"

The boy nodded. "A bandage. Roary would like a bandage."

William hurried to his office, carrying Golly in a pocket of his jacket. Miraculously, he did have some bandages in his desk. He poured some pop into a dish for Golly, then hurried back and performed a temporary repair on Roary. The lion lay still during the operation, but William could have sworn it winked at him once he was finished.

"I hope Roary learned a lesson." William wagged his finger in front of both boy and lion. "Fighting is bad. You shouldn't do it, and you shouldn't encourage others to do it."

The boy nodded. "I guess I should leave the ants alone, then."

An announcement blared over the intercom, reminding all the members that the office levels were closing. The boy's parents turned around. "Hayden, time to go!"

"OK." He looked up at William. "See you next year."

The lion flicked his tail at William as the family departed.

William put the rest of his insect collection back into his case, rearranging them so that Golly's absence was less apparent. Hopefully Golly would still be alive next year to greet this child when he came back.

William found himself looking forward to next year's Members Night already.

Caps in Red and Gray

After the tenth time Paul insisted on redoing a perfectly good take of "Back in the U.S.S.R.," Ringo complained, "Can't we just move on?"

"We've got to get it right! It could be the key."

Ringo set his drumsticks down. "To what?"

"Hopefully another limo," John muttered.

Paul glanced at George Martin and Geoff Emerick, then raised an eyebrow. No matter how long they'd all worked together, there was one secret the Beatles had never shared with Martin and Emerick. Sensing an unspoken signal, Martin and Emerick said something about getting tea and left the band members alone in the Abbey Road studio.

"It's your cap, Ring." Paul strummed a couple of notes on his bass. "It's got to be something about your drumming that's keeping it from being a proper red like ours."

"And ours have been ready for a long time," John said mournfully.

George crossed his arms. "We go as a group like we said we would, or we won't go at all."

Ringo felt under his shirt for his most precious family heirloom, a reddish-gray cap that had belonged to his great-grandfather.

* * *

When Ritchie's mum had given him the cap after one of his long hospital stays, it had been torn nearly in half.

"What does this have to do with medicine not working for me?" he'd asked. "Why did you keep something so old and worn out?"

"Cause you're not just human, son," Mum replied, stroking his hair. "You're also part merrow, by way of your great-grandfather."

"A what now?"

"A merrow. A type of mermaid, only in this case a merman. They used to take refuge among the humans, back when the docks were much busier than they were today. Me grandfather came ashore one day and fell in love with me grandmother when she was young and beautiful. Merrows need a cap like this to switch between human and mer forms, so she hid it from him so he'd have to marry her."

Ritchie frowned. That didn't seem nice.

"Grandma hid it so well, in fact, that she forgot herself where she put it. I found it after she passed away. Now it's yours."

Ritchie rubbed the cap. It felt like leather, and it smelled salty like the sea. How grand it would be to swim in the ocean and see what was below the surface!

He put it on. It fell over his forehead, and he didn't grow a tail.

"How come it doesn't work?" he asked.

"Maybe it needs to be made new again. Or maybe…" Mum frowned. "Maybe it's something to do with your dad."

"What about him?"

Mum seldom spoke about his dad, and this time proved no exception. She set about making tea and changed the subject. Ritchie put the cap away and told no one about it, until the day he met three other musicians who were also descended from merrows.

* * *

Ringo glared coolly at Paul, but his heart insisted on following an erratic rhythm. "There's nothing wrong with me drumming. My cap was just as battered as yours was back in Hamburg. It's gotten much better with all our music since then."

"Then how come it's still so gray?"

"Merrow caps are supposed to be red." John pulled a face, as if remembering his mother's legacy still grieved him after all these years.

"Maybe singing and drumming isn't enough. Maybe Ringo needs to write a song too," Paul said.

Ringo flushed, remembering the last time he'd brought a song to Paul and John and they'd howled with laughter before telling him which famous song he'd painstakingly copied.

"Then how come my cap was ready before yours, Paul?" George sounded smug. "It's something else, I'm sure."

Footsteps in the hall announced the return of Martin and Emerick.

Paul looked at his watch and said loudly. "We don't have time for 'Blue Jay Way.' The bridge needs more work."

"You can work on it yourself." Ringo stood, leaving his drumsticks behind. "Now I want tea."

It didn't matter how many takes they did per song, or how many songs they put on the next album. Ringo's cap hadn't changed color since the day he'd received it. Maybe there was something wrong with it, and it would never change him into a merperson. Maybe he should encourage the others to transform without him, no matter what they'd sworn in Hamburg.

***

October, 1960. Hamburg, Germany. Ringo and three of the Beatles had sat in on a recording session for Ringo's bandmate Lou. After the session, they'd hung out, drinking beer in the Kaiserkeller and listening to a set by another British group. They were all drunk, and John Lennon's insults about the current performers were the most outrageous things Ringo had ever heard. They talked and talked until Ringo felt as tight as a drumskin with John, Paul McCartney, and even underage George Harrison. When Lou finally left, the quartet felt even closer.

As George fumbled in his pockets for cigarettes, Ringo spotted a flash of brick-colored leather. "Hey, I've got one of those too!"

The other three sobered up, exchanging wary looks.

"What do you think it is?" George asked, a note of challenge in his voice.

"A...a cap."

Paul raised an eyebrow. "Where'd you get it from?"

Ringo realized maybe he shouldn't have let the beer talk. "It's nothing. Just a family heirloom. Rubbish."

John glanced around, then leaned closer. "Maybe not."

It turned out the three of them all had merrow grandfathers and great-grandfathers who'd left behind old caps, though his was the only grayish one. But what really got Ringo's attention was the revelation that singing or writing music repaired the caps and made them redder.

"We keep making music," Paul said, "And maybe someday the caps will be like new again."

"And we'll all go into the sea together," George added.

John raised his glass. "To the toppermost of the poppermost of the charts for the four of us, and then to the deepest of the seapest!"

Ringo wasn't quite sure what that meant, but as he drank, he knew he was joining a quest that was going to shape the rest of his life.

***

Ringo left the studio feeling despondent. The camaraderie of the early days was gone forever. Sure they'd gone to the top, but they'd never get to the ocean at this rate. He felt for the cap under his shirt. Maybe they'd all be better off if he left the group. The three of them could swim in the sea, and he…there had to be plenty of other bands that would welcome him, even if it wouldn't be the same. He tossed and turned the rest of the night, considering, before he knew what he had to do in the morning.

It might have been August, but Ringo's hands still felt clammy. He clenched them as he waited for John to answer the door. Ringo could have unlocked it himself—it was his own apartment; John and Yoko were borrowing it—but he had no idea what he would be walking into. When John finally appeared, his glasses sat askew, and his hair was a mess. Ringo doubted he had interrupted a composing session.

"What?" John sure didn't sound welcoming.

The words built up in Ringo's throat; when they finally came out, they did so all at once. "I'm leaving the band. I'm not playing well, and I feel unloved and out of it, and you three are really close."

John blinked at him. "I thought it was you three!"

"Pull the other one. I know better than that." Ringo waved his hand like a swimming fish.

Before John could respond, Yoko called him from inside the apartment. He turned toward her, and Ringo took the opportunity to slip away.

John's brush-off gave Ringo the strength needed to go to Paul's house and repeat his declaration, but Paul's reply was identical. Ringo would have thought they'd rung each other up, but Paul wasn't a good enough actor to fake that surprise. It must have been another sign from the universe proving that the others belonged together. There was no point in visiting George for a three-peat.

That's it, Ringo thought as he left. *I'm going on holiday, with me cap. And I'm not coming back until I know what to do to it.*

* * *

A yacht off the coast of Sardinia. Invitingly warm, though Ringo felt overheated after only a few hours. The water was so pure and blue Ringo wanted to dive in immediately. At lunchtime, he ate everything except octopus and learned about the local creatures. Octopuses were fascinating. Who would have thought they could build gardens under the sea? Maybe someday he would see it with his own eyes—or merrow eyes. For now, words and notes tugged at his brain, begging to be given a song of their own.

Ringo wondered what the others were doing without him. Had they made good on their threat to replace him? Would Paul insist on doing everything his way and alienate John and George too? Ringo shook his head and reminded himself he was here to forget about all that. But every time he saw the splash of a fish tail, he wondered if there were merpeople here. What could they tell him about merrows? Could he finish restoring his cap?

He could think of only one way to contact the merpeople: music.

Ringo waited until after midnight when his wife was asleep and the crew keeping watch elsewhere. Then he settled the cap on his head and hauled a portable record player onto the deck, along with a set of Beatles albums. He started with *Please Please Me,* the volume cranked as high as he dared. A pack of cigarettes kept him company as he studied the boat's wake, changing the records as they finished. Anyone watching him would assume he was remembering the Beatles' past, or perhaps contemplating the band's future. He couldn't help but compare how tight the four of them had been compared to the way things were now. *You'd think we've already been through enough together to bind us like brothers. What difference would it make if we all make that first plunge together or not? What if they've already done it without me?* For a moment, he considered waking the captain and telling him to take him back to England. Then he remembered how frustrated his mates had been.

He realized the music had ended. Ringo put on *Help!* and returned to the guardrail. A green-skinned youth with matching scales on his tail had climbed out of the water and clung to the side of the boat. Despite Ringo's excitement, he nodded casually to the merman so he wouldn't be scared away.

"What kind of music is that?" the merman asked.

"It's our music," Ringo said with pride.

"Who's with you?" The merman craned his neck. "You're the only Seaborn on this ship, but you're a mix if I ever saw one before."

"What do you mean?"

"You're not just one type of Seaborn. You're two."

"Two?" Ringo looked at his cigarette and sniffed it to see if it contained anything besides tobacco. "You mean there are more kinds out there besides merrow?"

"I don't know them all, since I prefer warmer waters," the merman said, "You're not from around here, are you?"

"I'm from England," Ringo replied. "Liverpool born and raised."

"Is that up north?"

Ringo nodded.

The merman rubbed his chin. "You must be part selkie, then."

"A selkie? What's that?" Ringo cautiously felt for his cap. "Does it have anything to do with merrow?"

"A selkie is a seal type of Seaborn." The merman studied Ringo's face. "That must be where you get your good looks from. Male merrows are notoriously ugly."

"Are they now?" Ringo wished his mates were here so he could rag them about that. "And do selkies need a cap to change, like the merrows?"

"No. They have sealskins. That's your trouble." The mermaid lowered himself until his tail was back in the water. "Ah, that's better. Anyway, where'd you get the cap from?"

"Me mum. It was me great-granddad's."

"So he must have been the merrow in your line. And the selkie? Do you know anything about selkies?"

Ringo shook his head. The selkie part might have come from his pa; it could have been what his mum had hinted at when he was a boy. But he'd never been close with his dad, certainly not close enough to ask about something this strange.

"Well, if you don't have a sealskin, you can't become a selkie." The merman descended further into the water. "And that part of your nature will always war with your merrow part, so the cap won't help you."

"Then what will?" Ringo peered over the rail. "Wait! Please, don't go!"

The merman was gone.

* * *

Ringo continued to stare at the water, but he didn't bother playing more music. Water lapped at the boat, taunting him. Why couldn't his mum have told him about his selkie background? Why couldn't his dad have taken an interest in him long enough to pass on that part of the family history, or better yet, a sealskin to go with it?

"Why should it matter if I'm both selkie and merrow?" he muttered at the sea. "I don't need to be a selkie the way I do a merrow."

The sea didn't answer him, so he returned to bed. Maureen slept heavily, but he dreamed of life underwater, chasing octopuses. Then a yellow submarine chugged by, with John, Paul, and George waving at him. He swam after them, but the sub left him behind. He woke up late, groggy, and annoyed. To force himself out of his lousy mood, he messed around with a guitar, trying to write a tune. As the day wore on, Ringo found sprightly chords that made him hum. No one pointed and said, "That's just like this song that was a hit ten years ago," so he kept at it. He needed words, though.

"Want octopus for lunch?" the captain asked with twinkling eyes.

Ringo shook his head. Maybe he could make this song to be about octopuses. He doubted anyone else had ever done that before. Then he wondered if anyone had ever written songs about merrow or selkie. He couldn't record it, but maybe if he sang to his cap and explained why it was so important that he go under the sea with his mates, it would understand. Could magic hats understand songs? It seemed no sillier than believing it could turn him into a merman.

Ringo continued working on two sets of lyrics, one for "Octopus's Garden," and one he privately called "The Red Cap of Merrows." As the charm of the holiday wore off, he struggled to finish the second song. Finally, the night before they were supposed to go home, it was done. He snuck out to the deck with his cap and his guitar. He set the cap in the middle of the deck and addressed it.

"Hey there, Cap. Mum told me you used to belong to me great-granddad. You allowed him to turn into a merman and swim in the ocean. Well, I know I'm not a full-blooded merrow like him. I'm also part seal, but I'm mostly human. A merman told me I can't turn into a merrow because I'm so mixed up inside. But I really need to become one." He cleared his throat. "You see, I have three mates, more like brothers, who are also part merrow, and we all swore we'd swim in the sea together. If we don't…." Maybe when he returned to Abbey Road, he'd learn they'd replaced him with a different drummer, the way he'd always feared. Or maybe they'd all decided to go their own ways and leave this album unfinished. As frustrating as recording had been lately, Ringo didn't want that to happen yet. "It's not fair that the different parts of me don't get along. If it wasn't for me mates being merrow, I wouldn't care what I was as long as I could swim with them. Anyway, Cap, I think music does you good. I hope you like this little tune I wrote for you."

He quietly sang,

I'd like to be
Under the sea
With the red cap of merrows on my head.
My mates and me
Have much to see
With the red caps of merrow on our heads.

He hadn't written as many verses for this song as he had for "Octopus's Garden." If what he'd managed to write wasn't enough, an entire song wouldn't do the trick.

My mates are fish
And so I wish
For a red cap of merrows on my head.
I'm part selkie
Don't have to be
With a red cap of merrows on my head.

He finished

I'd like to be
Under the sea
With the rest of the Beatles—and you.

He strummed a few more chores, then set the guitar down and picked up the cap. "So, what do you say?" he asked. "Can we go swimming sometime?"

He couldn't feel any tears, but there wasn't any trace of red left, only gray.

"Sod it! What went wrong?"

He'd have to let the boys know what had happened. Maybe it would be best to let them swim off by themselves. Ringo shoved the cap into his pocket, wishing it had a hole where the cap would stay hidden forever.

***

A few days later, Ringo trudged down the narrow lane to the ocean off the Scottish coast, where the rest of the Beatles had suggested they meet. Were they already here? He couldn't see them through the mist, but the tang of salt in the air guided him to the rocky beach. His mates stood at the water's edge, still clothed.

When Ringo was practically on top of his mates, he thrust his restored cap at them. "I sang it a new tune," he told them. "A real new tune. It did something, but--"

John peered at Ringo's cap. "It's still not red."

Ringo didn't point out the faint shadings that saved his cap from being a uniformly dead grey. "I found out I'm not just part merrow, but part selkie too. So the cap might not work for me after all. You guys should go for your swim without me."

"How do you know it's not going to work?" Paul asked. "Have you tried it yet?"

Ringo shook his head.

"It's worth a try," George said. "Come on. Even if it doesn't work for you, we'll keep you safe." He lowered his voice. "We all missed you back at the studio, you know."

"You really did?"

"You'll see." George grinned, giving Ringo more hope than he'd had since he'd sung to his obstinate cap.

John had already removed his shirt. Ringo wandered down the beach to give himself some privacy before taking off his clothes and stepping into the ocean. He waited until he was waist-deep before closing his eyes and settling his cap on his head.

A tingle spread from the top of his head to his toes. His legs bent in odd places as they fused together. Gray fur covered his arms, and webbing grew between his fingers. His chest bulked up. Only his head remained unchanged. He dipped his head below the water to view himself. The bottom half of him was pure seal, while the top half was covered with sealskin but still retained human shape.

Well, this isn't what I expected. It's strange, but…it feels right. Did the others change too? Do they look like this? He swam toward George. At first, Ringo thought George hadn't changed at all, but he seemed to be swimming faster than Ringo had ever seen him before. "I've got a tail, Ring!"

"So do I!" John came up behind them and hit the water hard with his tail, splashing them.

Paul came up last, staring at Ringo while trying not to appear as if he was. With a sigh, Ringo rolled over so the others could have a good look at him.

"I think you make a great mer-seal, Ring," George said. "You look a lot warmer than I feel!"

John nodded. "You know we love you no matter what you look like." His tone was honest, carrying none of his famous bite.

Ringo didn't trust himself to speak without bawling. It was good to know his friends accepted him no matter how strange he looked. It made it easier for him to accept himself, mixed heritage and all.

Paul pointed downward. "I think there's a shipwreck or two down on the bottom. Want to go check them out and look for treasure?"

"Yeah! Let's go!" Ringo replied.

He took a deep breath, noticing how much more air his lungs seemed to hold, then dove. As John, Paul and George followed him, he decided he didn't care if they found treasure or not. Their bond was the real treasure, something that would hold a little longer thanks to their caps of red and gray.

Blood for Sap, Sap for Blood

"Roots and leaves, we've lost another one!" Longleaf gently touched the dying oak, not even waist-high. Curled up in the heartwood was an infant dryad. The poor thing would never leave her tree, never roam in the moonlight with Longleaf and her sister dryad Redbark. Worst of all, she wouldn't be able to help them defend the University of Wisconsin from other supernaturals.

Redbark looked up from the mud she was studying. Thanks to the newly installed gas lamps on Bascom Hill, Longleaf could see several sets of human footprints in the dirt. "Can't you do something to help our daughter?" Redbark asked.

Longleaf shook her head. A few days ago, her green hair had been stubble, but it was finger-length. Soon it would be waist-length, copying the quick growth of leaves during this time of year. If a tree couldn't grow and thrive in springtime, what help could she give it?

"I don't think so," Longleaf told Redbark. "I've already brought the sapling water and checked the soil."

"If you take the dryad to the Grove—"

"She's not big enough to leave the tree."

Redbark slumped, letting her spear droop with her. "Then that's another failed acorn. What went wrong with the Great Marriage this time?"

Oak trees produced bumper crops of acorns every few years, during one of the Great Marriages. A dryad prince or king traveled to every dryad's tree to mate with her. Only certain acorns were capable of bearing dryads along with trees, and it seemed fewer and fewer acorns sprouted and survived after each Great Marriage. Longleaf and Redbark were the last dryads in the area. Where would the next generation of dryads come from?

"I don't know," Longleaf replied. "But we have to report this to Queen Brilliance-in-Fall."

"What if she refuses to let us plant another acorn?"

Longleaf stared towards State Street and the capitol building. Tethered to her tree, she couldn't leave university grounds, but she could see how the city surrounding the campus was growing. "The queen won't let a place of learning go undefended. Sooner or later, another dryad sister will join us."

"We could use her right now," Redbark said. "Look at this footprint, how deep it is compared to the others."

A footprint stood out in the patch of mud. It was larger than the other human male shoeprints, but deeper. Whoever had left it was several times heavier than the average human. That could only mean one thing: a supernatural in disguise.

"Do you think it's a dragon?" Now that she wasn't focused on the sapling, Longleaf noticed a faint trace of sulfur in the air. She glanced at the newly constructed Science Hall. A few years ago, a dragon had slipped past their guard, started a fire in the original building, and delayed the fire-fighters until it was too late. Thankfully, the dryads' trees were too far away to be caught by the flames, though the queen's tongue-lashing afterwards almost made Longleaf feel her death would have been preferable to failure. They couldn't let a second attack damage the campus again.

Redbark sniffed the ground, then raised her head and repeated the process. "The trail is several hours old. I think it extends past our tether."

"What doesn't?" If the campus grew, the dryads would be able to range farther from their trees without problems. In the meantime, they had to foil other supernaturals who wanted to sabotage this place of knowledge. "Only one of us needs to report the failed seedling to the queen. I'll do it so you can patrol the campus—and track down that dragon."

Redbark nodded and crept away, following the dragon's trail.

Longleaf returned to her tree for a leaf and then traveled to Library Hall. The way to the queen's Grove was always through a library. Her bare feet whispered as she passed between the long tables and headed for the shelves. Other trees had given up their lives to preserve knowledge. As long as her tree was healthy enough to put out new leaves every year, she would protect the remains of her people and the wisdom they contained.

Once she'd threaded her way through a maze no human could trace, she descended a flight of stairs that took her from the fresh air and light of Earth to the world of the Grove. It hadn't changed since Longleaf was a sapling. She nodded to the guard on duty. Longleaf spotted a lady-in-waiting and passed her leaf to her. "Longleaf Quern, guardian of the University of Wisconsin, requests an audience with her Most Gracious Majesty, Queen Brilliance-in-Waiting."

The lady-in-waiting smirked as she inspected Longleaf. On Earth, dryads seldom wore clothing unless they expected to encounter humans. Here in the Grove, the Dryad Court still copied fashions and manners humans had abandoned centuries ago. "You'll have to make yourself presentable before the queen will see you."

Longleaf nodded, having expected as much from previous Grove visits. In a changing room, she donned a velvet dress and arranged a fillet and wimple over her hair. Then she headed for the heart of the Grove, where the queen dipped her feet into clear pools of water and met advisors and petitioners. Longleaf curtsied and waited, head bowed, for the queen to acknowledge her.

"Rise, Longleaf." Queen Brilliance-in-Fall was three hundred years old and still in her prime. Like all other oak dryads, she had dark brown skin and light-green hair, in her case obscured by her ruby-studded crown. What set her apart from other dryads, besides her ornate robes and throne, was her sharp gaze and her height, being nearly seven feet tall. She outperformed ordinary dryads in other ways too. Not just one, but two of her acorns had sprouted into rare dryad princes. How sympathetic would she be towards her less successful subjects? Longleaf had never had an audience with the queen before, but from what she'd heard from other dryads, the queen was more willing to issue orders than genuine help.

"What business do you bring before our court today?" the queen asked. Behind her stood one of her advisors and the lady-in-waiting who had delivered Longleaf's token.

"Your Majesty." Suddenly thirsty, Longleaf fought the urge to dip her own feet in the queen's pond. "I regret to inform you that our last sapling is dying."

"Are you sure nothing will save her?"

"A dryad healer would know better than me, Your Majesty."

"A pity none are available." Queen Brilliance-in-Fall gestured at a pitcher of sugar water. "Especially since not all dryads have green thumbs."

The lady-in-waiting tittered as she served the queen.

"My sorrow at your loss, Longleaf. But tell me." Queen Brilliance-in-Fall leaned forward. "What happened to the rest of your acorns?"

Longleaf swallowed. "Only a few bore dryads, Your Highness, and they both failed to thrive."

"Roots and leaves, why?"

"I...I don't know, Your Majesty." Dare she say what she and Redbark had speculated about, that the last Great Marriage had failed? As one of the dryad princes, a child who appeared like a six-year-old human boy, ran to his mother, Longleaf realized she couldn't. The queen would point to her own offspring as proof to the contrary.

"Then I can give you no more acorns. They're needed in other territories." The queen turned away.

Longleaf waited, but everyone else ignored her, gushing over the precious prince. That gave her the anger and courage to speak.

'Roots and leaves, Your Majesty, two dryads aren't enough to guard the university, not when it's so close to the rest of the city and the state government! The area we have to cover keeps getting bigger!"

Queen Brilliance-in-Fall sniffed and reached for her drink. "You can't be certain of that, Longleaf. I've lived longer than you; I've seen people and places once thought important be forgotten like last year's leaves. Who knows what will happen to your university in another century? In the meantime, I must save all my acorns to replace dryads killed in the western territories." She waved her hand. "If your university needs you, you'd best return."

Longleaf knew she was being dismissed, but the queen's words stung so much she couldn't go quietly. "There's more supernatural activity in that area than you realize, Your Majesty."

The queen narrowed her eyes. "Then persuade one of them to aid you."

"Or better yet, turn a human into a dryad!" the lady-in-waiting said. "There's no many they'll never notice if one's missing."

The queen and all the other dryads within earshot laughed. Longleaf retreated, her parting curtsey perfunctory. Bad enough they refused to help her; they didn't need to mock her at the same time. Unless—she tramped through a pond and scattered water everywhere—what if a human really could be transformed into a dryad? All Longleaf needed was a tree, a human female, and a way to merge them together.

***

As Longleaf and Redbark patrolled the university grounds the next evening, they discussed what kind of human they wanted to recruit. Redbark suggested someone who already had a warrior spirit, someone who wasn't squeamish. Someone who appreciated learning as much as they did. Most important, it had to be a human they liked. All three of them would be together for a couple of centuries, and even the expansive university campus would seem as small as a leaf if they quarreled.

"She could go right here." Redbark pointed to a tree at the top of the hill, next to Bascom Hall. This oak had passed the sapling stage and was between ten to twenty years old. "It might be a tight squeeze at first, but it's a healthy tree and will give her at least two hundred years of life she wouldn't have otherwise."

Longleaf nodded. Humans seemed so fragile. Whoever they chose would be grateful for her extended life. But how could they pick one human female out of such a large group?

They crept over to Ladies Hall. The building wasn't as tall as the trees surrounding it, but it had four rows of windows and two rows of wooden porches and balconies. Young women smothered in gowns, gloves, and hats talked and laughed outside. Longleaf scrambled up a tree. A couple of the students pointed to the waving branches, but from their exclamations, they thought owls or bats were responsible. As Redbark joined her, Longleaf studied the women. Some were talkative and others quiet. Some seemed to dominate the others, and others made the women surrounding them laugh. But one woman in a mauve dress held herself apart from the others. She stared at the tree where the dryads hid, making Longleaf wonder if she knew they were there.

Redbark tapped Longleaf's arm and pointed. "That one. She's on guard duty."

Longleaf shook her head. "The human guards are older, and they worry more about keeping the males out of the building than supernatural attacks."

"Humans breed as if they have a perpetual Great Marriage." Redbark said. "I'm not surprised they need to control their males. But yes, I think that female knows we're here. The others carry on as if everything is normal, but she still watches. We should make her one of us."

Longleaf agreed the mauve-clad woman seemed the most likely candidate. But how did one approach a human? Their hair came in several different colors, not just green, and almost all of them had pale skin. Dryads couldn't pass as human—unless it was too dark for them to see each other. The last time Longleaf had been caught by a human, he'd chased her until she merged with her tree and hid for almost a month.

They couldn't risk frightening their potential new sister—especially if she then betrayed them to men with axes.

"We could disguise ourselves," Longleaf said. "Humans react better when we wear their clothes."

"It's better when we encounter them privately, not part of a group," Redbark said. "Let's invite her to the library tomorrow night. We can bring her to the Grove and have the queen tell us what to do next."

When full dark arrived, the women went inside. The mauve-dressed woman passed through one of the doors on the second floor. Longleaf waited until all the lights were out, then gestured for Redbark to follow her. They scrambled up the wooden beams of the balcony. The door was locked, so the dryads peered through windows. Redbark beckoned Longleaf over. "I found her." She pointed to a bed where a woman lay sleeping. The mauve dress hung on a hook in the wall. "Now what do we do? Should we wake her?"

"She might rouse the entire building. Let's write her a note instead." Longleaf retrieved a leaf from her tree and traced a message on it: "Come to Library Hall after sunset." She wedged the stem into the space between the wood and glass pane so her note was visible from the inside.

"Now we just have to wait until tomorrow night," she told Redbark. She hoped the woman was as brave as she had appeared to be earlier. It would take a courageous human to face the dryad queen.

* * *

During a thunderstorm, when all the students were huddled inside their classrooms, Longleaf slipped over to the young tree to prepare the twig.

"We've found you a possible dryad," she told the tree as she stroked its bark. "A dryad would look after you and keep you company. Since you weren't born with a dryad, we need something from you to bond with the human. Will you give me your straightest twig?"

After a few moments, branches rustled overhead, and a twig fell at her feet. As long as her finger, the twig was already stripped of bark, hollow, and pointed at both ends. Longleaf picked it up and wondered why the tree had shaped the twig before giving it to her. This was bigger than she had expected, almost weapon-like. She drew the tip over her skin. Clear sap welled up. *Am I supposed to bleed the human?* Longleaf wondered if she should take this twig to the lady-in-waiting and ask her for advice, but she realized now the other dryad had meant her suggestion as a joke. She probably didn't know what to do either. So Longleaf thanked the tree and brought the twig to Redbark, who had climbed high enough in her own tree to survey the whole campus.

"I don't like this weather," Redbark said. "There's a tinge of smoke mixed into the fog. I think the dragon has returned."

"Where is it?"

"It's not on campus now," Redbark replied, "But the smell of smoke is strongest near the library."

Longleaf sighed. "Of course it is. And on today of all days too. We're supposed to meet the human tonight. Maybe we should leave her another leaf and tell her not to come."

"No, don't." Redbark said excitedly. "This could be our chance to test her."

"Roots and leaves, Redbark, you can't be serious. Humans are no match for dragons. Besides, we don't know what to do with this." Longleaf pulled out the pointed twig.

"The queen didn't tell you what you should do?"

The queen had been more interested in her foot bath and sugar drinks than helping her, but Longleaf didn't tell that to her sister dryad. "I could go back to the Grove, but I don't know if I'll return before our meeting with the human," she said.

"You can't leave the campus. The dragon will certainly attack if you do." Redbark braided a lock of hair out of her face. "Maybe you should talk to our cousins."

It took Longleaf a few moments to remember who she meant. "You mean the naiads in the lake? If you gather flowers for them, I'll borrow a book from the library."

Redbark met her an hour later at the lakeshore, bearing garlands made with more dandelions than buttercups. Longleaf hoped the naiads wouldn't mind. As Redbark tossed the flowers into the water, Longleaf read out loud from a poetry book. Naiads appreciated such gifts. Eventually, a blue-haired, silver-skinned woman poked her head above the water. "What do you need of us, sister?" Water circulated around her as she pumped it through the gills on her neck.

"Can a human become a dryad?" Longleaf asked.

The naiad laughed for a few moments. Longleaf waited until she stopped.

"This isn't a joke?" The naiad brushed hair out of her eyes. "You have a human that wants to bond herself to a tree?"

"We haven't asked her yet," Longleaf admitted. "But Redbark and I need another sister to help us defend the books."

"Don't dryads grow from seeds?"

"Acorns. But they're not thriving."

"Nothing thrives when humans are about." The naiad scowled. "If you make one of them into a dryad, she'll only contaminate your race."

"They told me to do it at our court, but they didn't explain what to do. All I know is we need wood from the dryad's new tree, like this." Longleaf waded into the water up to her ankles, holding out the strange twig.

The naiad said nothing for several moments as she examined the twig. "You cannot change someone else to such an extent without changing yourself as well," she said. "Will you pay that price?"

"I don't even know what it is," Longleaf said.

The naiad sighed, as if dealing with a child that didn't know how to tread water. "If you want her to share your nature, you'll have to take on hers. Blood for sap and sap for blood." The tree sliver floated back to Longleaf. "Without the exchange, there can be no transformation."

With that, the naiad ducked back into the water and disappeared.

The dryads stared at each other. "Roots and leaves, Longleaf, you'd think the queen might have mentioned that minor detail," Redbark said.

Longleaf trembled as the full import of the naiad's words struck home. "It's...it's not a minor detail, Redbark. If we plan to make her a dryad, one of us has to become human."

Her sister dryad let out a short laugh. "But that wouldn't help us! We'd still only have two dryads, not three!"

"Then why bother doing it at all?" Longleaf asked bitterly. She didn't want to be parted from her tree and lose hundreds of years of life. Redbark might be a brave warrior, but she wouldn't sacrifice herself so foolishly either.

Before Redbark could answer, students began to emerge from the lecture halls. The dryads bolted up the closest tree, where they would be safe from discovery. A pair of males passed directly below them, talking about mathematics. Redbark found an old acorn and prepared to drop it onto one of the student's heads, but Longleaf, listening in, reached over to stop her.

"Hold on, Redbark! We've been thinking one of us would have to exchange all of her sap for the mortal's blood. But there's two of us. What if we each give her some of our sap? It might be enough to change her while keeping us dryads."

"That might work." Redbark eyed the twig. "Since it's your idea, you can try it first."

Longleaf didn't answer, despite her relief at a possible solution. They still had to persuade this human to become one of them.

* * *

Longleaf and Redbark, magicbane-tipped spears in hand, approached Library Hall at sundown. The stench of dragon polluted the surroundings, but a perimeter check found no signs of entry. Redbark climbed onto the roof while Longleaf hid near the entrance. As the gas-lights came on, a woman hurried toward the library. Although she wore a different dress, she was the woman they had chosen last night. She tried the library door several times before creeping around the building and pressing her face against every window she could reach. Longleaf stole out of her hiding place and crept up behind the human.

"Betsy?" the woman called. "Where are you? Why did you leave me a note after all this time? And why put it on a leaf in the window?"

Longleaf deliberately snapped a twig underfoot. The woman nearly jumped into the air as she whirled around, wide-eyed.

"I'm not Betsy." Longleaf hid her spear behind her back. "But I'm the one who left you the note."

"Who are you?" The woman backed away, even though that brought her up against the building. "Dear Lord, what are you?"

"A dryad."

"A dryad? Like someone who lives in a tree?"

"Who is a partner to a tree," Longleaf corrected. *Roots and leaves, do I have to explain everything to her? How am I going to persuade her to become one of us?* She studied the human, so odd-looking with her brown hair and ornate clothes. She knew almost nothing about the woman. Maybe she wasn't a good choice.

Redbark dropped to the ground so silently only the flash of movement warned Longleaf of her presence. "Why did you come here, if you didn't know what dryads are?"

The woman's eyes went wide. "I thought you were Betsy, my…my friend. My very good friend." Her voice caught, and Longleaf wondered what kind of friendship it was that caused such hurt. "It was nice to meet you…."

Longleaf knew enough about human custom to guess this woman wanted to leave. The longer she could keep her talking, the more likely she would stay with them. "I'm Longleaf, and that's Redbark."

"How pretty. I'm Victoria Stout." Shyly, as if she thought they weren't interested, she added, "I'm studying history."

"What part of history?" Redbark asked.

"European, but I've love to learn more about ancient civilizations." Victoria looked wistful. "There's so much we still don't know about them."

Longleaf and Redbark glanced at each other. Victoria seemed just as interested in learning as they were. She would probably love having a couple hundred years to listen in on any lecture given on campus.

"Do you like the university?" Longleaf asked.

"I love it here!" Victoria replied. "There's so much more freedom here than there was back on my family farm. I'm lucky to have an aunt willing to sponsor my education, even though my father says no one will want to marry me once I'm done with all my learning." She glanced back at Ladies House. "Well, I'd better return to my room before anyone realizes I'm gone—"

The moonlight dimmed as a shadow passed overhead. Sulfur-tainted wind attempted to push Longleaf and her companions away from the library. She curled her bare toes, as if that would be enough to anchor her this far from her tree.

"What is that?" Victoria gasped.

"A threat to books and learning, better known as a dragon," Redbark answered grimly. "It's our task to defend the university from creatures like him."

"You should go now, while we deal with the dragon," Longleaf told Victoria. "They're dangerous."

She expected the human to flee, or perhaps break out in hysterics. Instead, Victoria hid behind a dryad-less tree, then peered out to watch, a stick in her hand. Another point in her favor.

The dragon tucked in his wings as he landed, rear legs touching down first. He shifted into a heavyset human male in a black silk suit. He must want something if he was willing to talk before attacking. Longleaf still brought her spear around to have it ready the instant he charged.

"What do you want?" she asked.

"Such courtesy." The dragon sneered. "My territory is vaster than a tree-bound creature like you can comprehend. It takes me days to travel from one side to the other. You could at least offer me refreshment."

"You'll have to wait until morning for sunlight," Redbark snapped.

"I didn't come here for sunlight." The dragon turned from one side to the other, surveying the campus. "I'd rather finish what I started."

"Were you the dragon who tried to burn down Science Hall?"

"I see they rebuilt it. How annoying. Every generation, humans keep breeding and breeding. Soon, there won't be a single corner of the globe that's free of them."

Longleaf couldn't help but smile at the dragon's mixed metaphor.

"I don't know why you think that's so amusing," the dragon said. "Even I can tell there are fewer trees here than there were the last time I came. What makes you think your trees are safe? Join our side, dryads, and help us push these invaders back."

The dragon must not have known much about dryads if he thought they were going to sympathize with him. Yes, humans did take up more than their share of space, and they thoughtlessly changed the world to suit only themselves. If they learned about dryads and other supernaturals, they would probably try to exploit them too. Yet Longlegs felt more kinship with humans than she did with dragons. Humans destroyed things, but they also created knowledge—and their ancient religions had brought dryads and all the other supernaturals to life in the first place.

Longleaf hefted her spear. "The only one we're going to push back, fire-breather, is you. Knowledge is sacred and should be protected. Leave now before we stab you with magicbane."

"I'll break you all like twigs!" With a scowl, the dragon lowered his arms. His form blurred as he expanded back into his natural shape. Before he could complete the transformation, Redbark darted forward. If she managed to prick him with magicbane, he would be stuck in human or half-human form, leaving him vulnerable and less able to damage the library. It was a strategy that served dryads well.

It didn't work for humans, who were slower than supernaturals and didn't have a magic-cancelling chemical smeared onto the ends of their sticks.

The dragon, still half-shifted, lunged past the dryad to attack the human. As he passed Redbark, she pivoted to land her spear in his human posterior. The wood poked out of his trousers like a poor substitute for his spiked tail. The dragon's face was elongated into a snout, with a couple of fangs. His hands had already changed completely into clawed feet, and he raked Victoria from shoulder to waist. Five streaks of blood welled up from her shredded dress.

"Victoria!" Cursing herself for her slowness, for inviting the human here, for everything, Longleaf thrust her own spear at the dragon's face. Her focus narrowed in to his yellow-green, vertically slit eye. Piercing it with her spear was the most natural, effortless thing she'd ever done. He pulled away before her blow could kill him. With an unearthly howl, he covered his face and fled on foot.

Longleaf should have hounded him to the end of her tether, to kill him or ensure he never returned. Instead, she stared at the bright red blood welling up from Victoria's body. Roots and leaves, there was so much of it, and it kept on flowing. That couldn't be good.

"So much blood. Is she going to lose it all?" Redbark asked as she knelt next to Victoria. She gave Longleaf an odd look. "Are we supposed to give her sap now?"

Blood for sap, sap for blood. The naiad's words came back to Longleaf with new meaning. Maybe if they replaced Victoria's blood with sap, she would become a dryad. What would happen to them?

Despite all the pain Victoria had to be feeling, her eyes were still open, and they stared at Longleaf, asking for something she wasn't sure she could give.

"Please...I want ...." Victoria reached for the twig.

"You want this?" Longleaf asked incredulously. "You want to be like us?"

The human mouthed something that looked like "yes."

There would be time for formal oaths to protect the university later. Longleaf jabbed one end of the twig into her wrist. It took several tries, as her skin was resistant to being injured by wood. Finally, with a fierce jab and a splintering sound, sap welled up from her wrist. She smeared sap on Victoria's wounds to close them. Longleaf put one end of the twig into her wrist and the other end into the final slash on Victoria's chest. Redbark held the twig in place.

As sap left her, Longleaf became lightheaded. She watched Victoria's face become pale, and the dryad thought that they'd failed and had lost her. Longleaf's arm burned inside, the sensation traveling slowly but steadily throughout her body. It took all of her willpower not to jerk away from the twig. The human's blood must have entered her own body. Was it fighting to change her?

New sensations flooded her: feelings of hunger only satisfied by chewing and swallowing food, not absorbing nourishment from her tree; of being muffled by scratchy clothing when she wanted to run free; pain and illness too. But she also experienced the contentment of resting at the end of the day, having helped bring in the harvest or bringing home game for dinner. The taste of her mother's apple pie; singing hymns in church; the happiness of being part of a family at the holidays.

These are Victoria's human feelings, not mine. Longleaf tried to shake the memories away. Such fleeting moments they were, not like the slow seasons she experienced with her tree. But they complemented the conversations between students that she overheard every day. She understood what it meant to Victoria to leave her family and come here. All the excitement and fear felt a thousand times stronger than anything she'd ever experienced. The freedom and passion tempted her to break her bond with her tree so she could dance in the humans' streets.

"That's enough." Redbark grabbed the twig, but Longleaf wrapped her hand around Redbark's so the other dryad couldn't steal it from her. How could she go back to her slow-paced life of watching others and defending the territory when she had a human's blood in her veins?

"Roots and leaves, Longleaf, listen for your tree. Your tree needs you."

The human's frenetically-paced memories ebbed, unveiling the steady, deep rhythms of Longleaf's tree, patiently stretching for the sun and enduring season after season. Her tree. Her anchor, her other half. She couldn't abandon it no matter how much the human world called to her.

Slowly, Longleaf released her hand and let Redbark take the twig away. It was hard not to feel a pang of jealousy as Redbark shared her own sap with the human. Already Victoria's skin had a brown tint to it, and her hair showed traces of green at the roots. The sight of Victoria as dryad helped restore Longleaf's own sense of identity, She wandered down to Lake Mendota and drank until her head cleared, then she scooped up a handful to bring back to the others. Redbark appeared caught up in the same experiences that had nearly trapped Longleaf, so she threw the water in her face. As Redbark blinked, Longleaf pulled the twig out of her arm, then Victoria's wound. She placed the twig, swollen and marked with dryad sap and human blood, in Victoria's hand and curled the barely aware woman's fingers around it. The vivid red of the blood made Longleaf realize the sun was rising. Humans would be about soon. Best to hide Victoria before her former companions searched for her.

"Do you think the tree will accept Victoria?" Redbark asked.

"We have to try." If the tree wouldn't take her inside itself, all of this had been for nothing.

Redbark grabbed Victoria's shoulders; Longleaf, her feet. Together, they hauled her up Bascom Hill and set her down next to her designated tree. As soon as Victoria brushed against the bark, she fell into the trunk and disappeared.

"Well, that's that." Redbark sounded more satisfied than triumphant. "She'll need some time to bond with her tree. Best to leave her in there for a while."

Longleaf nodded. Without a word, she headed back to her own tree. The sweet scent of new leaves welcomed her, chasing away the iron tang of human blood. Yet, as Longleaf stroked the bark of her tree, she noticed a slight tinge of pink in her brown skin. Maybe she would carry some human traits with her long after her body replenished her sap. Still, as she glanced over where Redbark's tree stood, then up at Victoria's, she didn't regret her choice.

All three of them were bound by sap and blood, wood and flesh, and would be together as long as their trees flourished. Together, they would keep the university safe.

Henry's Harness

Hannah placed the photo of Henry in front of his ashes to block her view of the urn. She hesitated before laying his harness next to it. It didn't belong on a mantel, but around his neck as they were working.

Maybe it would be better if I kept it in my laptop bag. That way, I'll always have him with me.

She folded it up and tucked it into a side pocket, where no one would know it was there. Few people, not even her ex-husband and grown-up kids, understood the bond between a tracking bloodhound and his human. Even her priest had looked at her oddly before blessing the harness. She'd raised Henry from puppyhood and taught him how to track missing pets. Over the years, they'd handled about fifty cases, some ending happily and some with sad resolutions. She'd expected Henry to have a few years to enjoy retirement, but the cancer had spread too quickly. Maybe once she'd paid off the veterinary bills, she could consider adopting another bloodhound. Hannah doubted she'd ever find one as tenacious as Henry.

Perhaps his death was a sign she should give up her volunteer work as a pet detective. Her boss, State Representative Jane Burnett, had only hired Hannah after her last assistant had gone back to northern Wisconsin to deal with family problems on the reservation. If he returned, Jane would probably prefer someone from her tribe over a new employee with an unusual hobby that took her out of the office at odd time. Hannah sighed. Giving up tracking and working with dogs would be losing something that made her feel truly alive. But without Henry by her side, tracking would never be the same.

* * *

Hannah straightened her suit jacket before entering the assembly chamber in the Capitol. The air conditioning felt like ice coating her skin. Worse, the room smelled like fish, as if someone had deliberately placed tuna sandwiches by each of the vents. A couple of the representatives, including Jane, were already in their seats, taking calls or typing on their laptops. Jane preferred reading printed documents, so Hannah had to run a couple of reports over from the office.

While she waited for Jane to let her know if she needed anything else, Hannah glanced at the podium. Normally her attention was drawn to the painting that occupied the wall above the podium and woodwork, but today she studied the bird perched at the gilt border. When she'd first started working here, Jane had explained that the bird wasn't real, but a replica of a famous bald eagle named Old Abe. He'd been a mascot for Wisconsin soldiers during the Civil War and had lived at the Capitol after the war. Unfortunately, he'd been a victim of fire twice—once when smoke inhalation had led to his death, and a second time when his body had been destroyed in another fire in the building. All that was left to remember him was this statue.

Jane looked up. "Hannah, I hate to make you run back and forth again, but could you get my cardigan? It's cold in here today."

"Sure, no problem." At least she didn't have to stay for the entire session.

Ten minutes later, the room was filling up. Hannah handed over the sweater, then surveyed how many people were watching the proceedings from the third-floor gallery. Today's session included bills on water usage, dairy regulations, and the ever-popular topic of taxes. Audience members included a group of kids on a field trip, a couple of journalists, senior citizen activists who had time to analyze every nuance of bills and amendments, and a blonde college student snapping pictures of the chamber with her phone. As she leaned forward, her pendant swung away from her. Hannah had never seen anything like it before: a glowing glass jar. Must be something trendy among the younger generation. Hannah wondered if the security guards had inspected it. However, the jar appeared too small to be a threat.

"Oh, no." Jane groaned.

Hannah turned back to her boss. "What's wrong?"

"Steinmetz introduced a bill to take down all the information at Camp Randall about the Civil War. I guess he thinks we can't talk about it at all."

"Maybe he's a sore loser."

Jane grinned briefly before gesturing to keep quiet. Steinmetz was originally from Georgia. Despite living in Madison, Wisconsin for over twenty years, he still harbored many Southern attitudes but was no Southern gentleman. Both Jane and Hannah tried to avoid being alone with him.

"At least we have Old Abe to remind us about our history," Jane said. She gestured toward the podium. "Sometimes I feel as if his spirit is still here."

Hannah nodded and rummaged in her computer bag for a pen. She brushed against the harness. It felt as warm as if she'd just removed it from its owner.

Jane stared at the bird for a few seconds before typing some notes in her file. It looked like she was going to invoke the old war eagle in her speech opposing Steinmetz's bill. Leaving her to it, Hannah returned to the office.

* * *

"I hope they close the chamber tomorrow," Jane announced when she returned from the assembly. "There must be something wrong with the air conditioning. It's colder in there than it is on Lake Mendota in January."

Hannah murmured sympathetically and checked the herbal tea stash, in case they had to bring her a fresh hot mug every hour during tomorrow's session.

"What's worse is that Steinmetz's bill is still alive," Jane continued. "I can't believe people are willing to support it." She sighed and shook her dark hair out of its clip. "Then again, in today's world, anything is possible, I suppose."

Hannah bit back a gasp as the harness bumped against her side. It felt as if it was moving around on its own—or like Henry was wearing it.

Jane raised her eyebrows. "Something wrong?"

"No, I'm fine." Hannah plastered a smile in place. "But I can't stay too late tonight. I have to get home to Henry—I mean…"

"Go on, take some time." Jane waved her away and spread some graphs on the top of her desk. "We're not voting tonight."

Hannah ordered a meal for her boss before leaving, just to make sure Jane ate. As she passed a restaurant on the Capitol Square, the smell of burgers wafted out. The harness twitched in her bag.

What is going on here? She'd suspect a prank, but she'd kept the harness concealed all day. No one else knew about it. She hurried back to her townhome, worried the harness would either embarrass her or worse, get itself lost and sever her last link with her favorite bloodhound.

Back home, she laid the harness in the center of the kitchen table so she could watch it during dinner. It only took her a few minutes to pull leftover pasta, salad, and a bottle of wine from the refrigerator. As she poured a glass, Hannah glanced over at the table. The harness was no longer there. She peeked around the kitchen island to see it on the floor.

No, not the floor. Hovering above it, at just the same height it would be if Henry was sitting there, watching her.

Hannah reached for the wine glass, then paused before touching it. Whatever was going on here, she didn't need to confuse things with alcohol. "Henry?"

The harness bounded toward her. She heard something click, like nails on linoleum. Tentatively, she reached out toward the harness. Cold surrounded it, but her fingers didn't contact anything solid.

"Henry," she whispered. "Is that you? Did you come back to me?"

Dust seemed to swirl as if the air was stirred by something—a wagging tail, perhaps.

Hannah cautiously stroked the cold shape somehow holding the harness in the air. She recognized every curve of the canine form, the feel of Henry's fur beneath her fingers. She didn't need to see him to identify him. How had he returned? Hannah didn't think anyone could explain this miracle. It didn't matter. Her best friend was back again, and she needed to make the most of every second with him.

"Henry. Such a good boy you are." Her voice sounded rough, but she didn't care. She embraced the cold spirit as best as she could, trying not to lean on Henry too much for fear of crushing him. He tolerated the hug for a while, then finally pulled away after Hannah's stomach grumbled.

Before eating her own dinner, she rummaged through the pantry, looking for leftover dog food. She'd given most of it away, but she found a box of Henry's favorite treats. "Do you want Liverbonz?" she asked, holding it out as if their nightly ritual had never stopped.

The harness approached the treat, but it didn't disappear.

Of course he can't eat it, you fool. He's dead. You're imagining this.

She reached out again. The leather harness felt real, a little rough on the edges from wear. It was still surrounded by cold. Her imagination had never been this tangible before.

She scratched behind Henry's ears until her fingers grew numb. As Hannah blew on them, she had to admit this was real, even if she didn't understand how or why Henry had returned to her. Feeling like she was doing something greatly daring, she took Henry on a stroll around the block. It was too dark for anyone else to see the floating harness. Part of her felt as if Henry had never left, but fear he'd disappear made her cut the walk short. She'd never been more relieved to come back inside and see the harness still suspended in mid-air.

She streamed a movie before bedtime, scratching where Henry's ears would be until her fingers felt frostbitten. The harness floated next to her knees, as if Henry was waiting for an assignment. She wondered what a ghost dog could track. Another ghost? On a whim, she switched to the *Ghostbusters* remake, but Henry didn't seem interested. She went to bed wondering what to do with him.

* * *

Trapped in such a small space. Unable to see, unable to watch over the room where he'd spent such a long, long time…

Hannah woke half-convinced her arms were wings; her blanket, a trap preventing her from flying. She struggled to toss it off. Cold landed on her stomach. The sight of the harness floating in the air brought her back to herself and the surprise from last night.

She sighed as she scratched Henry's ears. "Henry, you know you're not supposed to be in bed." Or in this plane of existence, for that matter. "Get down."

He jumped down and followed her from room to room as she got ready for work. As she dressed, she wondered what she should do with him during the day. What were a ghost dog's needs? If he didn't need to eat, he probably didn't need to be walked. Would he be here when she returned home, or would his harness be lifeless again? She wished she could bring him into work, but a levitating harness would cause chaos. If she tried to remove Henry's harness, would she be able to find him again? She wouldn't leave it on a living dog this long, but Henry had always perked up when he wore it. It was much more a part of him than his collar and tags had been. Would his ghost even exist without the harness? Losing him once had been hard enough; she didn't want to endure it twice.

In the end, Henry decided by blocking the door. "I can't let people see your harness floating like that," she told him. "You'll have to hide."

She tossed a Liverbonz into an oversized shopping bag. The harness dove in, reminding her of games they used to play. The bag didn't rustle as Henry laid down inside. His coldness protruded past the heavy paper, but thankfully the bag didn't seem damaged. Even more good news was that Hannah could carry the bag easily. If Henry's ghost had weighed a hundred pounds as he did when he was alive, she wouldn't have made it out of the house with him. She covered the harness with an extra sweater for additional concealment during the bus ride and walk to the office.

"Good idea bringing in some more clothes," Jane said when Hannah arrived. "If the chamber is still an icehouse today, I predict a short session."

Surprisingly, it wasn't super-cold, but super-hot in the chamber. The security guard raised an eyebrow at the extra sweater but waved her through after pawing through the bag. If he felt Henry when he touched the harness, he didn't comment.

Jane nudged her. "Why is your bag moving?"

Hannah bit back a curse and pulled the bag closer, hoping no one else had noticed. The bag quivered as if Henry had found a scent trail and was ready to work. What could he be scenting? There were no other animals or remnants of animals here, unless you counted leather, which Henry had been trained to ignore. The closest thing to a representation of an animal was the statue of Old Abe. It seemed tarnished today, the paint worn, the eyes dull. How had that happened overnight?

As more people filed in, both in the chamber and the viewing balcony above, Hannah pulled out the documents Jane needed for today's session. She wondered what it took to make a dead animal return as a ghost. Maybe Henry had come back because he knew she still needed him. Or maybe he had a mission of his own. Old Abe had been famous for his Civil War service. In a way, the statue was a Civil War memorial, just like the ones being torn down in the South. Maybe someone had defaced it in revenge.

Hannah studied the podium during the opening remarks. There was no sign of damage, and no one else in earshot had commented on Old Abe's bedraggled appearance. Maybe she was imagining it. She was certain by now she wasn't imagining Henry. If he could rejoin her, what other impossible things were real?

Something nudged her leg. She looked down to see the harness had crept out of the bag and was edging toward the podium.

"Henry, no!" she whispered.

He didn't listen. Another foot or so, and his harness would be in the center of the aisle, visible to everyone.

She lunged for the harness and grabbed it. Hooking her fingers under it, she hauled Henry slowly back to her. He resisted as if he weighed twice as much as he had in life. *Next time I take him anywhere, he'll have to be on a lead.* She commanded him to heel several times before he obeyed. "Now, stay!" she whispered. Her legs grew cold, then gradually numb as the session dragged on. But she couldn't leave. Jane watched her with intent brown eyes. Hannah's cheeks flamed.

Henry must have found a trail he wanted to investigate. To find out what it was, she'd have to return here when no one else was around. To do that, she'd have to explain everything to Jane and hope she believed her.

* * *

"We seem to be blessed with a spirit companion," Jane remarked when they returned to the office. "Could you tell me more about him, Hannah?"

She placed an order for pizza. As Henry explored the office, Hannah told Jane everything: how she'd trained him to find lost animals, the searches they'd undertaken, his death and unexpected return. She even told Jane what she'd noticed about Old Abe's statue.

"I've never encountered anything like this before, but I agree something strange is going on." Jane wiped tomato sauce off her chin. "I didn't like the feel of the chamber today. Maybe it was because of the heat, but everyone was more disagreeable than they normally are. Except for Steinmetz."

"Well, he must be used to heat." Relieved her boss believed her, Hannah helped herself to another slice. She automatically picked off a piece of sausage for Henry before remembering he couldn't eat it. "Seeing as he comes from an infernal place and all."

Jane grinned. "Don't say that in public. I don't think my constituents would care, but the press might." She became serious again. "Normally I wouldn't expect so many other members to listen to Steinmetz, but if the eagle guardian is missing, I think they're more susceptible to his influence. Meanwhile, your hound's spirit has returned to you, and you've been having strange dreams. You don't need me to interpret these signs, Hannah. You and Henry are the only ones who can track Old Abe—"

Her phone buzzed. She frowned as she read the text.

"You'd better find the eagle's spirit soon," Jane said. "Steinmetz's bill comes up for vote tomorrow."

Hannah swallowed, the cheese seeming to stick in her throat. "But how can Henry pick up Abe's scent when there's nothing physical of Abe left?"

Jane shrugged. "You're the pet detective, not me. Time for you to become a spirit detective as well. But I do have an idea..."

* * *

Hannah hid in the shadows outside the Capitol as she clipped a twenty-foot lead onto Henry's harness. Her fingers tingled. The night was balmy, but her hands were anything but.

As she waited for Jane to return, she circled the building and tried to think like an eagle-napper. How could you capture one, especially a spirit? How would you hold it, and where would you take it? Was it more important that she was tracking a bird or a ghost? Hannah pulled out her phone and searched for information on both, mentally cursing the slow Internet connection. She halted when she read eagles ate mostly fish. *Maybe that explains the foul odor in the chamber the other day.* If nothing else, fish might make a good substitute scent article for tracking a bodiless spirit.

She searched for "ghosts" and nearly let out a groan when she realized how many times it was mentioned online. "Trapping ghosts" proved to be more relevant. One time-honored method was to put a lit candle inside a glass jar. Not even Jane would be allowed to use lit candles inside the assembly chamber. Hannah suddenly remembered the glowing pendant the spectator had been wearing the other day. Maybe that had been the trap for Old Abe.

Jane emerged from a parking garage as Hannah rounded the corner. "I have it," she said. "You may look at it, but don't touch it. It's sacred."

"Touch what?"

Jane pulled a long, narrow wooden box from her tote. She knelt and slowly opened the lid. Inside, on a bed of satin, rested a single plume. Attached to it were beadwork and a leather cord.

"I'm honored to be the carrier of this eagle feather," she said. "It was a gift when I was first elected to office, as a reminder I should follow the Seven Grandfather Teachings no matter where my path led me." She glanced down and quirked a smile. Henry's harness floated forward. "This bird that bore this feather was born long after Old Abe, and certainly not a descendant. But I pray to the Creator that it will guide your companion tonight."

Jane seldom spoke about her religious beliefs. As a Catholic, Hannah might not have believed what Jane did, but she knew this was a special honor. She bowed her head and said, "Thank you."

Jane lifted the feather out of the box by its cord. She carefully dangled it in front of her, keeping it clear of the sidewalk. The harness inched toward it. Hannah could picture Henry stretching his long muzzle toward the scent article, nose quivering. When he'd been alive, it had never taken him long to acquire the scent. Now, he lingered as if he was an untrained puppy again. Hannah let the lead hang loosely in her hands and watched the harness. When it finally turned away from the eagle feather, she held her breath. Henry's harness cast about from side to side. Hannah swallowed a lump in her throat. It was just like before Henry got sick, when the two of them were a team. But she'd never undertaken a missing pet search like this before. There were no physical signs she could follow, no one she could interview for possible sightings. She was wholly reliant on Henry and his supernatural nose.

Henry abruptly chose a direction. Hannah let about three-fourths of the lead run through her fingers before following. It was odd not seeing Henry's liver-and-tan back. She was glad he'd never given voice when he was on the trail, as it made the lack of sound from him more bearable.

Henry stopped at the entrance to the garage where Jane had parked. "I hope I didn't confuse him with the feather." Her whisper sounded like a shout despite the noise from a passing car.

Hannah shook her head. "He's casting about for the scent again."

Henry didn't proceed into the parking garage. Instead, he headed straight into the street.

"Henry! Danger!" Hannah pulled on the lead, but she encountered more resistance. Henry had weighed around a hundred pounds when he was at peak health, and it felt now as if he'd carried every single one of them into the afterlife.

A car engine sounded behind them. Hannah pulled desperately on the lead. Somehow, she got Henry, harness, lead, and all, off to the side just before the car whizzed past them. A male student leaned out of the passenger window and yelled something—thankfully unintelligible—at them. Hannah stopped to let her nerves calm down. Maybe it was foolish to think a car could hurt a ghost, but she didn't want to risk losing Henry again. She gathered up about half of the lead to keep him closer to her.

The trail led up several blocks. Just as Hannah was wondering if Henry would wade into Lake Mendota, he veered to the left. Apartment buildings gave way to fraternity and sorority houses. Music and lights blared from several of them. Short-skirted girls carried cups of beers from one house to another. Hannah grimaced as the smell of beer overwhelmed her. How did Henry cope with it?

"You didn't pledge during undergrad, did you?" Jane asked. "I never bothered to rush."

Hannah shook her head and pulled the lead up to keep Henry close.

Henry led them to one of the quieter sororities—quieter in the sense that there weren't a hundred college students milling about. He tugged her from the driveway to the street and back again. She tried to avoid staring at his harness, in case someone noticed.

One of the young women came up to them with a stack of cups. "Ten bucks for...oh." Hannah felt all the disdain someone young enough to be her daughter could put into a single syllable.

Henry pulled forward with renewed determination.

"Oh my god!" Another girl shrieked and sloshed her drink. "Look at that! It's floating!"

Jane stepped forward. "It's just a trick, girls. It's not a ghost."

Hannah groaned. *Don't plant thoughts in their heads, boss.*

"Too bad Rachael's not here," the girl with the cups said. "She'd probably think it was real."

"Oh, is she into ghosts?" Jane asked in a fake-casual voice.

The second girl nodded. "All sorts of old and dead stuff. Matter of fact, she said there was something going on at Camp Randall tonight."

Hannah and Jane exchanged glances before Henry tugged a few feet of lead out of Hannah's hands.

"Cool trick!" the first girl called after them as they hurried on.

* * *

By the time they arrived at Camp Randall Stadium half an hour later, Hannah regretted insisting they walk the entire way so Henry could confirm the trail. Jane had changed into sneakers when she'd gone home for the eagle feather, but Hannah still wore her office heels. Blisters made her vow to keep a casual outfit and a pair of loafers at her desk, in case Henry ever brought her on another nocturnal hunt. Despite her protesting feet and the chill in the air, she felt exhilarated. On previous pet searches, she'd always tried to temper her thrill in the hunt in case it ended with a dead animal or inconclusive evidence. She knew she wasn't going to find any remains here. What would she find? If Rachael did have Old Abe's spirit trapped in her pendant, what could they do about it?

"You should leave," she told her boss. "This could affect your re-election chances if we're noticed."

Jane shook her head. "My people will understand. There are some things more important than politics."

Hannah doubted that the ghost of an eagle, no matter its history, was among them. Before she could reply, Henry surged forward, nearly tearing the lead out of her hands.

Jane halted and signaled for Hannah to do the same. "I think I saw a shadow move," she whispered.

"Where?"

"By the arch."

Hannah strained her vision. It took her a couple of moments to realize that it was too dark. "What happened to the lights?" she asked.

"I don't know. Maybe somebody covered them, or smashed them."

A speck of light flared near the gate. As they drew closer, Hannah could see it was inside a pickle jar. A woman-shaped silhouette held the jar above her head.

"I don't believe it," Jane whispered. "This used to be a training ground for Wisconsin soldiers during the Civil War. She must be collecting their spirits."

"Are a lot of them buried here?" Hannah asked.

"No, but this is the historic site. She's stealing the power from this place too, just like she did to the Capitol."

"We should call the police." An anonymous tip, and they could catch a taxi home, no way to connect them to whatever was happening. But what would happen to Old Abe?

Jane laughed bitterly. "They wouldn't listen to us. You know that."

Henry impatiently tugged at his harness. The lead hung in the air, as steady as a ruler. Then the tension disappeared. Lead and harness fell to the ground.

"Henry!" It took all of Hannah's restraint not to scream his name.

He let out a series of howls as he bounded toward the lighted jar. The woman froze. Hannah rushed toward her, instinctively following her dog.

The woman swiveled, thrusting the jar at them. The votive candle inside slid around but remained burning. Henry's cry cut off mid-note as the harness broke. Hannah drew close enough to confirm it was the blonde student she remembered from a couple of days ago. Rachael— if that was her—gloated as she capped the jar.

She's got Henry in there. It was all Hannah could do not to snarl herself. "Give me back my dog." She glared as hard as she could at this student, wearing clothes more stylish than anything she could ever afford.

"What dog? I don't see any dog. Do you?" Rachael spoke with a soft drawl. She widened her eyes, but she couldn't keep the glee out of her voice.

"You darn well heard him just now."

"You're imagining things." Rachael drew herself straight, as if she thought she could intimidate Hannah into leaving. She shifted her grip on the jar. Its light already seemed dimmer.

You'd think a college girl would be smart enough to realize if you cover a candle, it'll burn out. Hope she's not a science major. Hannah tried to keep her expression neutral. She hadn't had time to research what would happen if Rachael's candle went dark, but she'd bet it would hurt the girl more than the ghosts. She just had to keep her distracted for a couple of minutes.

"You mean, like I imagined you visiting the Assembly Chamber the other day?" she said. "The day you stole our resident eagle spirit in your pendant. How'd you get it to glow? Does it have an electric light?"

"I don't know what you're talking about," the girl said as she raised a hand to her throat. Yes, the light in the candle was dying. Just a couple more minutes...

Hannah stepped forward. Rachael wrapped her arms around the jar, leaving only faint glows from the top and bottom visible. If Hannah were twenty years younger and had more faith in her joints, she would have considered tackling the girl. At her age, words and emotions were a more reliable weapon.

Hannah crossed her arms in a near-mimicry of Rachael. "See, what I don't get is why you care so much about a war that ended over a hundred and thirty years before you were even born. Your side lost. Get over it."

"No, your side lost the last election." Rachael sneered. "We're back in charge now. Soon the whole world will know the truth about the War of Northern Aggression. Then we'll be where we belong, on top, and you'll be scrubbing floors on your knees...."

The glows died. Hannah held her breath, waiting for something to happen. Seconds ticked by as Rachael continued to hug the glass jar. Where was Henry?

"Don't think I'm stupid enough to free your dog." Rachael backed away. "I'll hide him somewhere where you'll never find him and come back some other time for the soldiers."

Maybe she should have tackled the girl after all. Only one more thing Hannah could do, the one thing that had drawn Henry's attention no matter what trail he was following. She took a deep breath and yelled, "Henry, Liverbonz!"

The jar trembled. Rachael hugged it to herself, but then she gasped and dropped it. She shrieked as shards of glass peppered her skin. Hannah ran forward. She'd never felt so glad to encounter a spot of cold before. She fumbled in her pocket for crumbs of Liverbonz. If she couldn't reward Henry with a real treat, at least he could enjoy the smell.

"Where's the eagle, Henry?" she asked. "Where's Old Abe?"

It was too much to hope the bird had been freed along with Henry, but Hannah waved a hand in the air, searching for a spot of cold above her head. How well had the eagle flown when he was alive? Maybe he would take off for the Capitol or the wild, and she'd never know what had happened to him.

Henry danced briefly to her hand, but he evaded her before she could reattach his harness. Rachael staggered back as if pushed. "Ow! Leave me alone!" She swatted at the air, at the spots of blood on her arms, at the necklace she wore. It was the same one she'd worn a couple of days ago.

Jane stepped out of the shadows. "Release the eagle spirit," she intoned. "And perhaps you won't suffer much more for your foolishness."

Rachael stared at her. Hannah tensed. It was so tempting to tackle her and rip the necklace free, but that could get her put in jail—and possibly ruin her boss's reputation. What else could she do if Rachael didn't listen?

Rachael grimaced. "Stupid bird isn't worth keeping anyway." She yanked at the cord, getting it tangled in her wild hair before finally working it free. "I'll have better luck with real ghosts. Here."

She held out the necklace, but before Hannah could take it, Rachael threw it toward the arch and ran in the other direction.

"Should we go after her?" Hannah asked her boss.

Jane shook her head. "We can't press charges or do anything else to punish her. She'll end up punishing herself. Let's see if your dog can find the eagle again."

Hannah practically turned her purse inside out before she found a chunk of stale Liverbonz. It was enough to distract Henry while she draped his harness in place. He found the necklace in less time than it took Hannah to extract it from a bush. As she'd guessed, a tiny electric light powered by a watch battery made the jar glow. Cords had been wrapped over the jar to keep the lid in place. The necklace was so cold it burned her fingers. If Hannah was going to continue working with

Henry, she'd need to invest in flexible but warm gloves before she lost a couple fingers to frostbite.

"I think you should hold Old Abe," she told Jane as she passed the necklace on to her.

Jane smiled as if she guessed Hannah's true motive. "What now?"

Hannah bit back a moan as her blistered feet complained. "Uber. Or a taxi. Whichever is faster and less likely to think I'm a crazy woman with a floating harness."

* * *

Hannah staggered as she left the taxi in front of the Capitol. Her emotions had had time to play out during the short ride, but she kept focusing on one thing: she could have lost Henry again. What would have happened to him if she hadn't been able to rescue him from Rachael? What was she supposed to do with him now? Was he supposed to cross over the Rainbow Bridge, like it had said on a poster in the vet's office? She hadn't a clue how to find it.

Jane retreated to a quiet nook, chanting softly as she held the tiny jar by its cord. When she stopped, she searched in her tote for a small toolkit and pulled out a pair of pliers. "For crafting," she explained to Hannah. She struggled for a couple of moments to twist the lid off the jar. Hannah wanted to help, but she didn't think Jane would accept it. Finally, the lid flew off. Jane staggered back a couple of steps. A whoosh of artic wind brushed Hannah's cheeks.

"Abe?" she whispered.

Her ears tingled with a screech almost beyond the range of her hearing.

The current of cold flowed away from them. "Any idea where he's going?" she asked Jane.

Her boss shrugged. "I told him he was free to rejoin the Great Spirit if he chooses. I'm not sure if he understood me. We'll find out tomorrow—well, later this morning—if he returned to the assembly chamber instead."

Hannah hoped so. It would be a relief to have the room temperature—and people's tempers--back to normal. Maybe then Steinmetz's bill would fail to pass.

Jane pulled out her keys. "Do you want a ride home?"

"Just a minute." Hannah knelt. The harness hovered by her left leg as Henry maintained a perfect heel position.

"What do you want, old boy?" Her voice sounded a little rough. Must have been the stress of the night. She stroked his icy ears, telling herself it might be the last time she ever did so. "Do you want the Rainbow Bridge?" She trailed her chilled fingers down to his harness. "Or do you want to stay with me?"

She pulled the harness away from him. "No matter what, Henry, you'll always be a good dog."

She waited. A cold spot bumped her face. She let out a shaky laugh as a cold tongue attempted to lick a tear from her cheek.

"I take it he's not leaving," Jane said.

Hannah settled the harness over Henry. "Though I don't know what I'll do with a ghost tracker."

"Teach him to track more ghosts." Jane's expression grew solemn. "And if you have to clean up piles of ghost dog poop, leave them in Steinmetz's seat. He'll never know."

The two women laughed as they walked back to the parking garage with Henry's harness by Hannah's side, where it belonged.

But Not Today

A sister. Gwen needed a sister, someone to make the nursery feel less lonely.

It was a very nice nursery, befitting a noble family. Although it was on the top floor of the manor, so tall Gwen's short legs ached after climbing all the stairs, it was warm in the winter. During the summer, Dama s'Ren, Gwen's governess, would open windows at each end of the nursery to let cooling breezes pass through. Whitewashed walls reflected light, and colorful rugs and blankets made the room look lively. Cloth dolls to cuddle and porcelain ones with real hair and their own clothes, blocks and puzzles well-worn by previous lo Havil children, and picture books all promised plenty of hours of playtime. But Gwen never enjoyed playing by herself, and she wasn't good at it. She had too many memories of grown-up cares filling her six-year-old mind.

Gwen had memories from her previous lives because she was a Spring Avatar, born on the first day of spring. A long time ago, the Goddess of Spring had given Gwen healing magic. When Gwen grew up, she would find the other three Season Avatars her age, and together they would tame Chaos Season, the magical storm that mixed up the seasons. She wished they were here right now so they could play together. Even if they were boys, like the child Mama was carrying and was going to name Grant.

Poor Mama had been trying to give Gwen a brother or sister for years. Finally, last year, she'd made a special trip to the capital city of Wistica to see the current Ava Spring. Gwen had pleaded with her parents for days before they'd agreed to take her too. They hadn't been sure the current Avatar would want to meet her successor. But she'd been very kind to Gwen, asking her if she remembered the One Oak, the big house where all of the Avatars lived, and telling her it was all right that her magic wasn't active yet. "You need to use your energy now to grow big and strong so you can help others later," she said. "And now I need to see your mother privately so I can help her."

Mama had gotten with child the next moon, so the Spring Avatar must have healed whatever was keeping her from having another one. Gwen wished the Avatar could have come to their country estate for the birth. Mama had started having pains yesterday, and Gwen hadn't been allowed to see her since. How could her governess insist she practice her Fip verbs as if everything was fine? No one had told her anything.

If no one will tell me what's going on, I'll have to find out on my own. She would get in trouble if she was caught outside of the nursery. But the more Gwen thought about it, the more convinced she became she should escape. Maybe she didn't have magic for Mama yet, but she had lots of memories about helping women have babies. Of course, she didn't understand them very well, but she could explain them to the midwife and let her do the work.

Gwen tried the door handle, but it didn't budge. "Freeze it," she muttered, glancing around to make sure her governess hadn't heard her. Young noblewomen weren't supposed to swear. Had Dama s'Ren locked her in? How was she supposed to get out? Gwen wasn't a Summer Avatar with magic that worked on plants and wood. She barely had any magic except her memories and ability to see the colors of other people's auras. Maybe one of her memories would give her the answer.

She sat in the rocking chair that was just her size and thought about doors and locks. She remembered a lot of doors from the One Oak were so old there was only one key for them, so the key was kept next to the door, or even in the lock, so it wouldn't get lost.

Gwen knew how to get the key—if it had been left in the lock.

One of Gwen's favorite things to do was draw. Dama s'Ren had given her a sketchbook and colored pencils for her birthday. Gwen carefully tried to push the sketchbook under the door, but it was too thick. She bent it back so only the cover stuck out, then slid that through the crack. Next, she took her least favorite colored pencil—orange—and tried to stick into the lock. The pencil was too thick, so Gwen had to sneak into Dama s'Ren's desk—another naughty deed—and borrow a knife to shave strips of wood off of the pencil. *Goddess of Spring, don't let the knife slip.* Even if her magic worked, she wouldn't be able to reattach her fingers if she cut them off.

When the pencil was so thin she feared it might snap, Gwen inserted it into the lock, pushing forward until she heard something fall on the other side. She pulled her sketchbook back, grinning when she saw the nursery key caught on the edge. Now to see if it would work from this side.

Gwen eased the door open. Every squeak sounded like the rumble of thunder, guaranteed to bring her governess running. Gwen poked her head out first. If her feet were still in the nursery, she couldn't get in trouble for leaving. No one was visible on the landing or on the stairs. A memory of being locked out prompted her to slip the sketchbook between the door and frame before venturing farther. The sketchbook had the extra benefit of softening the sound of the closing door.

She waited a few more heartbeats before gliding down the stairs. Her slippers whispered quietly on the wood. She knew the steps well enough so she could keep to the edges where the boards were least likely to squeak. Still, her heart hammered from more than the movement. What would she do if someone saw her? A servant might not tell on her, but Dama s'Ren would take Gwen straight to her father. He might forbid her from riding her pony for a whole moon.

As long as my mother is safe, and the baby, Gwen prayed. *Just let me see them for a few heartbeats. If they're well, I'll go back before anyone knows I've left.*

She finally reached the second floor, where her parents lived. When she was old enough, she'd have a room down here too. No servants were in the main hall, but at the first sound of voices Gwen crouched next to a big green vase honoring the God of Summer.

"The bleeding hasn't stopped," Dama s'Ren said. "Where's that raspberry leaf tea? Why isn't it helping?"

"You need to give it more time, Dama," a strange woman said. Judging by the timbre of her voice, she must be old, much older than Mama and Dama s'Ren.

Dama s'Ren lowered her voice, but Gwen's sharp hearing still picked out the words, "Lady lo Havil doesn't have time to wait."

Gwen clenched her fists. Every instinct in her screamed to rush into her mother's room and heal her. But her magic wasn't ready yet.

I have to try. For Mama, and the baby. Was her little brother all right? The governess and the old woman hadn't said anything about him, and she hadn't heard him cry. Maybe he hadn't been born yet, but if Mama was still in labor, she would be making more noise. This part of the house was too quiet. Something was wrong, and that meant Gwen had to do something to help. The question was how to do that without getting into trouble. She had to figure out how to get her governess and the healer to leave her mother alone so she could slip into the room. Could her memories help her with that?

Gwen closed her eyes and searched through her memories for a similar situation. She couldn't find one. All of her memories came from times when she was already grown up and accepted as a Spring Avatar. She couldn't think of an instance when someone had blocked her from treating someone else…

No, that wasn't true. A few centuries ago, soldiers from another land called Fip had crossed the Salt Waters to take over Challen. Gwen had been a man named Gabriel, and he and the rest of his quartet protected their country and helped everyone they could. One day he'd come across a group of wounded enemy soldiers. The Summer Avatar, Jasmine, hadn't wanted him to heal them. "They're the enemy!" she said, clinging to his arm. "If you help them, they'll only go out and kill more innocent Challens!"

She made a good point. But Gabriel was sick of seeing any wounded, no matter what side they were on. Even the memory of foul-smelling wounds filled with pus was enough to make Gwen nearly gag. She put her hand over her mouth to keep herself silent and forced herself back to the memory.

"We've already tried everything short of killing them outright," Gabriel said. "It doesn't matter. Everyone suffers, Jasmine."

"You could end their suffering with a single touch."

Yes, he could kill them, but then more soldiers would come with their foreign weapons more powerful than anything the Challens had. Worse, the Fip army was led by their own God-touched Avatar, and the Fips worshipped the God of War. The War Avatar had the uncanny ability to find the best spots and times to pitch a battle, and no matter what bad weather the Season Avatars sent him, no matter how they controlled the plants and animals in his area, he still advanced deeper into Challen. How many more moons could they resist, and how many more would die on both sides? Gabriel was heartsick of people dying because he couldn't get to them in time.

"We could stop all suffering if we end this war," he said. "Maybe if I heal these men, we could parley with the War Avatar."

Jasmine gasped. "You would talk terms with the Avatar of a foreign God? Would the Four approve? Or the king?"

"I don't intend to surrender the country," Gabriel snapped. "But maybe we can come to a truce so we have more freedom to move about and treat the wounded."

Kerry, the Avi Winter, shook his head. "Or they would try to capture us."

Gabriel hesitated. In some ways, the Season Avatars had been more effective defenders than the Challen army. But sometimes you had to take a risk…

"Sometimes you have to take a risk," Gwen repeated out loud as her mind returned to the present. She had to go out there and talk to Dama s'Ren and the strange woman so they would let her help Mama.

"What was that?" Dama s'Ren asked. "Is someone there?" Footsteps rounded the hallway.

Gwen stepped out from behind the vase, wishing she could mute her heartbeat. In front of her stood her governess. Despite the warm day, not a hair had slipped from her tight chignon. The silver chain for her spectacles glittered against the storm-cloud-gray dress. "It's me, Dama."

"You mean, 'It is I,'" the governess said. She raised her glasses to her hazel eyes. Dama s'Ren was slightly older than Gwen's mama, with a long face and thin arms that didn't go well with her green summer-born aura. "By All Four, Lady Gwendolyn, how did you get down here?"

Gwen took a deep breath and raised herself to her full height. She still barely came to Dama s'Ren's chest. "I came here to help my Mama, Dama. Please don't send me back to the nursery. I promise I won't take the key again."

An older woman with a winter-blue aura peeked from around Dama s'Ren. This woman had more gray hair and wrinkles than Gwen's governess, but her joints didn't creak, so she was healthier than she appeared. Brown smears on her rough dress smelled like blood. Too much blood. Gwen knew she couldn't let herself be scared by blood, as she'd seen plenty of it in her earlier lives and would handle more when her magic woke up, but now she wished she'd stayed in the nursery.

"This is the young Ava? How adorable!"

Gwen didn't dare forget her manners in front of her governess. The midwife was a commoner, but she was old enough to deserve respect. Gwen sank into a perfect curtsey. She raised her head and stared straight at the midwife. "Dame, please take me to my mother. I want to help."

The midwife put her hand in front of her mouth. "By All Four Gods and Goddesses! Little Ava, do you really have magic at such a young age?"

She drooped. "Not yet. But I can still help. You mustn't let a new mother bleed too much or get sick, or else she might die."

The midwife and Gwen's governess exchanged glances. "I can bring her back upstairs if she's a bother, Dame Trev."

"No, she's no bother. It's just—should she see her mother like this?"

"Dame Trev, I remember a lot—" At Dama s'Ren's frown, Gwen corrected herself—"I mean, I have a great many memories from my previous lives as a Spring Avatar. I may remember a way for you to help my mother. Please, let me try."

Dame Trev sighed. "I could use an Ava Spring right now. Very well. Come with me, little one. I mean, Ava."

At last, a chance to help. Gwen lowered her head modestly, but inside she felt like shouting with glee.

The midwife led Gwen down the hall to her mother's bedroom and rapped on the closed doors. "Lady lo Havil? You have a visitor. I'm sure she'll make you feel better."

"Who is it?" Her mother's voice sounded weak. Gwen wanted to dash in and heal her, or bury herself in her mother's arms. Mothers weren't supposed to be weak. They were supposed to be strong and perfect, everything Gwen wasn't.

"Your daughter." The midwife's voice sounded odd, as if she didn't want to announce Gwen.

"Gwen? She's here?"

Gwen couldn't wait any longer. She pushed at the heavy doors with all her might. They swung open slowly. Impatient, she edged through before her governess could scold her for unladylike behavior.

Her mother sat upright in bed, supported by a couple of pillows. Her blonde hair, a shade darker than Gwen's own, had been piled and pinned on top of her head, but several strands had melted onto her face. Her face looked colorless compared to her pink silk bed jacket. Bitter herbs and burning candles couldn't cover the scent of blood in the air.

"Mama!" Gwen edged closer to the bed, hoping her mother would invite her to climb up and snuggle next to her for a while. That only happened when they were completely alone, when even the servants couldn't see.

"You mustn't disturb her, child," the midwife said. She reached for Gwen, as if to pull her back.

"Leave her alone, Dame Trev." Gwen's mother raised her hand briefly. "As a matter of fact, leave us alone for a while."

"But Lady…"

Gwen's mother made a shooing motion with her hand, so faint Gwen almost didn't catch it. Then she collapsed back on her pillows.

Dame Trev studied both of them, a grave expression on her face, her lips pursed as if she'd eaten a lemon, rind and all. Then she left, pulling the door shut behind her. Gwen wondered if she'd have the strength to open it herself. But in the meantime…Mama smiled and patted the bed-cover.

Gwen hooked a foot between the mattresses and boosted herself up. The smell of blood grew stronger, along with an unfinished mug of willow bark tea. Blue wool blankets felt scratchy under her hands, more appropriate for winter than the summer day outside. Despite the blankets, Mama's hands were so cold Gwen pressed them between her own. Neither of them wore gloves, letting Gwen really *feel* how her mother was doing.

It wasn't just that she'd bled too much during the birth itself. She was still bleeding more than she should, and Gwen couldn't make it stop. She wanted to scream and pound the blankets, but she didn't want to disturb her mother—or the silence. It was too silent, even for a baby, and she didn't see the newly repainted cradle

"Where's my brother?" she asked, looking around. If he was here, he must be sleeping soundly. She knew he wasn't in the nursery. Maybe they had placed him in a kitchen window so he could soak up sunlight.

Mama's gaze became flat. "Gwendolyn, I'm so sorry, darling, but the God of Winter took little Grant back."

She sat up straight, indignant. "He took him back? How? Why?" She hadn't been able to sense much about the baby, but he'd seemed fine enough the last time she'd touched Mama.

"Something went wrong during the birth. I don't know what—it all happened so fast. So much pain…. He'd already gone before he arrived. Thank the Four he didn't suffer."

Gwen scowled. Why bother letting her mother bear a baby if the God of Winter wouldn't even let him draw a single breath? It wasn't fair! She would never understand the Four Gods and Goddesses, no matter how long she served Them.

"May I see Grant anyway?" Gwen asked.

"Ask Dame Trev. She said she'd find a white blanket to wrap him in."

Goddess of Spring and God of Winter I hope you give Grant a good sleep and a gentle rebirth. After praying for her brother, the only thing Gwen could do was turn her attention to her mother. "You must get better," she told her. "Eat all of your meat, and take the medicines the midwife gives you."

Her mother smiled slightly. "Thank you, daughter. At least I know you never have to be told to eat everything on your plate. I've always been very proud of you." She kissed her with thin, cool lips. "Go and play now, Gwendolyn. I need to rest."

Gwen wished she had her magic right now, so she could help her mother. *I should pray to Spring. She'll have to give me my magic early.* "Rest well, Mother," she said as she slid off the bed. "I'll be back soon."

Gwen pleaded with the midwife to let her see her brother's body. Poor Grant looked like he'd been carved out of ice. Gwen blessed him with a touch, then allowed her governess to escort her back to the nursery. Dama s'Ren scolded her all the way, but Gwen only paid enough attention to make the proper responses. As soon as Dama s'Ren locked her back in the room—the key scraped against metal as the governess pulled it out of the lock—Gwen knelt next to the window.

"Goddess of Spring, hear my prayer," she said. "Please, please, please let me have my healing magic now so I can save my mother. I promise I'll be the best Ava Spring ever."

She waited expectantly. Perhaps magic would surge through her, or it would build in like a fire slowly rising from kindling. How long would it take? Her mother didn't have much time.

Nothing happened for the rest of the afternoon. Gwen couldn't focus on the book Dama s'Ren had assigned her; drawing held no distraction. A maid brought up a tray with her dinner, but for once Gwen had no appetite. Gwen tried to put off going to bed as long as possible, but her governess had been with her long enough to know all of her tricks. As Gwen suffered Dama s'Ren steering her toward the bed, her energy drained out of her. She dragged herself onto her stepstool and on top of the bed and fell asleep before her head touched the pillow.

She found herself in a spring meadow. Flowers studded the grass, and songbirds courted their mates. A merry brook burbled through the meadow. A mother duck and her brown-and-yellow ducklings paraded up and down the brook as they searched for food. Gwen wanted to run about and roll in the grass, but she settled for nodding approval of perfection, the way her mother accepted each dish the servants presented to her during a soltrans dinner.

"Do you like My home, My daughter?" a woman's voice said behind her.

Gwen spun around. The woman in front of her shared her blonde hair and fondness for yellow clothing, but Her eyes were shadowed so Gwen couldn't look into them, let alone tell what color they were. Gwen still knew who She was.

"Goddess of Spring!" Gwen ran to her, only halting when she realized it might not be a good idea to hug a Goddess, even in a dream. "Did You bring me here to show me how to heal my mama?"

"Gwendolyn, My daughter. Walk with Me."

She hadn't answered Gwen's question. Either She wasn't going to, or if She did, She was going to do it like a grown-up and make Gwen figure out the answer herself. Some of Gwen's pleasure in the meadow faded, but she joined Spring on Her stroll anyway. One didn't refuse the Goddess who had given you magic.

Spring led them on a path by the brook. The meadow gave way to an apple orchard. The trees were in full bloom, and violets carpeted the space between each tree. Gwen paused to take a deep breath.

"It smells wonderful here, doesn't it?" Spring asked with a smile.

Gwen nodded. "I love apple blossoms. They're so pretty."

"Do you love eating apples as well?"

"And fresh apple cider, and pies."

"But you can't make apple cider or apple pie from flowers, can you?"

Gwen frowned as she stared at the trees. Not a single fruit in sight. Of course, she knew apples couldn't be picked until late summer or fall, moons after the last petal had withered.

"If it stays spring wherever You are, Goddess, does that mean You never get to eat apples?" she asked.

The Goddess laughed. The sound was as warm as sunlight. "Child, I never need to eat unless I wish to! But if I wanted apples, Summer could grow them for Me from these blossoms." She gestured at the trees. "All of these flowers would have to change before they can develop into fruit. The same goes for you, Daughter."

"What?" Gwen glanced down at herself to make sure she hadn't sprouted petals.

The Goddess laughed again. "You're not a flower; you're My Avatar. I think you'll become a fine one, perhaps the one who will help end Chaos Season. But before you do, you need to grow strong."

"That's why You don't allow us to use our magic when we're young." Gwen looked down, studying a bee tracing a path from violet to violet. "But I know I can do so much more, Spring. I remember it. Every day brings another memory. Why can I remember magic but not use it to save my mother? It's not fair!"

"It's not meant to be fair."

Gwen glanced up, still unable to meet the Goddess's eyes.

"I know you want to save your mother, and it's never easy for Winter and I to end a life, no matter if that person is very young, very old, or somewhere in the middle. Humans can't live forever. They need time in Winter's domain to reflect on what they learned before I send them into other lives."

"My mother has a very good life right now!"

"Only she can say that for certain. Right now she's very tired and unhappy. She knew she was risking her health if she tried to bear another child, even with My daughter Margaret's help. If your mother lives, she won't be able to have any more children, and that will make her unhappy for other reasons. She will be happier in her next life, I can tell you that much.

"As for you, My dear daughter, you won't remember most of this talk when you wake up. But you'll know your mother is at rest. She wouldn't want you to blame yourself or be unhappy, Gwendolyn. She and I expect you to grow up into a caring, compassionate Avatar. You won't want other people to suffer or lose their loved ones. You'll be the most determined of all of My Spring Avatars for having gone through this. You'll be strong enough to heal yourself and others, even in the most hopeless of cases."

The trees shimmered, as if the air had thickened.

"It's time for you to go, My daughter." Spring made the sign of the Four over Her heart. "Remember if you love someone very much, you may see them again in another life. Someday, years from now, you'll meet your mother again. Your sister Avatars, too. Be strong, Gwendolyn, and remember I'm always with you. You're never as alone as you think you are."

"Alone…alone…"

The word echoed, this time in a different voice. Gwen strained to recognize it, and in doing so, woke up completely. She sharpened her hearing. Dama s'Ren was whispering to someone outside the nursery door. "The poor child will be all alone now without a mama."

Gwen knew instantly what had happened. A sharp stab of grief faded as if it'd been smothered. *She's wrong. I'll see Mama again someday. In the meantime, I'll never be alone.* Gwen sniffed, hoping for the scent of apple blossoms. She would have sworn by the Four that she'd just smelled them…somewhere out of reach…

It was gone, along with the rest of her dream. She sighed, then rose and crossed over to the cabinet where the dolls were kept. A dozen of them, some porcelain, some cloth, waited for her.

Somewhere out there—she wasn't sure how she knew—were three other girls her own age, waiting to grow into their magic. Someday all four of them would be together, but for now, dolls would have to stand in for the Summer, Fall, and Winter Avatars. Gwen picked the three prettiest ones, wondering if they looked like the real girls.

"Someday I won't need you," she told the dolls as she set them around a table to drink chocolate. "But not today."

Last Locomotive from Wistica

Kay knew she was dreaming, but her terror was still real.

She plummeted from an unnatural height. Branches reached from below, waiting to rend her apart. She grabbed every breeze within reach to slow her descent. Dorian, the current Winter Avatar, hung suspended in mid-air from nothing but his own magic. He sneered as she fell past him.

"You're useless, Kay Seltich." The air carried his words to her ear. "If you were worthy of your weather magic, you'd be able to save yourself. You'll never be able to tame a Chaos Season, even if you find the rest of your quartet."

The branches grew closer. She frantically tried to steer herself away from them—

"Such a weak Key you are," a woman's voice added. "And doomed."

Another set of branches grabbed her. She shrieked—

And found herself in bed, huddled between her siblings. Safe.

Her heart pattered faster than the rain splattering through the open window. Thunder rolled above like the God of Winter speaking to her. She wished she understood His words.

Goddess of Spring, God of Summer, Goddess of Fall, and God of Winter, that's the third time I've dreamed of falling. If the nightmare returns, will it come true?

The Four Gods and Goddesses of Challen wouldn't let her die at fourteen, would They? She was one of Winter's Avatars, gifted by Him with weather magic so she could sort out the mixed-up weather of Chaos Season. In a few years, when the Four signaled it was time, Kay would lay down her needle and join with three Avatars her own age.

They'd replace the current quartet, and she'd live in the One Oak and send chals to her family. If she didn't die first.

Kay extracted herself from her sisters and knelt by the window.

Send me a sign, Winter. Tell me what I must do.

The window rattled as if inviting her to open it and crawl outside. She shuddered. There was a tree outside with branches almost big enough to hold her. After that dream, she planned to keep her feet on the ground.

"Kay…Kay…"

An apparition floated outside her window. Dorian? It certainly looked like the Winter Avatar, a blonde man who appeared decades younger than his true age. His sapphire suit fit him perfectly, but the color made his eyes crueler. Kay crossed her arms over her brown-gray dress. The blue swirls she'd embroidered on the cuffs didn't show how threadbare the fabric was.

"Join me if you dare." He smirked. "Or stay here forever."

He couldn't be real, she told herself. The current Avatars had no reason to seek her out so soon. She had to grow up here in the Winter Quarter of Wistica and learn how to help the common people. Besides, no Winter Avatar was powerful enough to fly on the wind.

Unless…was this Winter's answer to her question? Maybe He was testing her. If she wasn't able to overcome her fear, she wasn't worthy of serving Him.

Kay grasped the window latch, then hesitated. Something didn't seem right. Why would the God of Winter test her with Dorian's image? For hundreds of years, she, Dorian, and a third Winter Avatar named Olivia had taken turns guarding the country of Challen. Although their names and genders changed from life to life, Kay always recognized Dorian when they encountered each other. It didn't matter if she was his student or teacher; he always treated her with contempt. Why would Their God make them spend more time together than necessary? Besides, Dorian was still alive, while Olivia's spirit was in the God of

Winter's domain. She was more suited to being Kay's mentor than Dorian.

"Very well, stay here." Dorian coated the window, including the broken pane, with ice. "You're not ready for this challenge. I'll wager my place at the One Oak that you can't even melt this frost."

She knew he was goading her, but she didn't care. Her moonflow had arrived this spring, and with it, the magic she'd been born with surged to life. During the day, she was so busy helping her mother with sewing that she never had a chance to practice using her magic. Like a wayward wind, her magic wanted to be free.

Directing warm air at the window was as simple as willing it to happen. Water beaded on the glass and rolled off. Soon Kay had a clear view of Dorian again. Still no sign of approval or even acknowledgement of her talents from him. *After all these lives, I should know better.* She wasn't a second-class Avatar, but he always made her feel that way.

Scowling, Dorian shoved a gust of wind at the window. The glass shattered. Kay deflected the shards with a counterblast of air. She managed to protect her face, but her arms stung in a dozen spots. With the window entirely open, the wind howled in like a rabid animal even the Fall Avatar couldn't tame. Kay balked. How could she manage this? She knew she'd tamed hurricanes and whirlwinds before, but that was in past lives, when she was linked with the other members of her quartet. Now she was young, with new magic and no other Season Avatars to work with.

Wind poured through the opening, bringing cold. The wind tugged at the single blanket her sisters shared. They huddled together even in their sleep. Kay might not be bothered by the cold, but they were.

How dare Dorian threaten my family! He's never stooped that low before. Anger drove Kay out of the window and onto the nearby tree branch before her fear could stop her. Bark dug into her bare feet. She clutched other branches as the one she crouched on groaned. Dorian laughed and floated higher, out of reach.

By the Four, what do I do now? She ought to hurl lightning at her rival, or cover the broken window so her family would stay warm. The best she could do was direct the rain away to keep them dry.

The wind ceased for a few heartbeats. Then it pummeled her from all directions.

She pushed against the winds, but they'd already done damage she couldn't mend. The branch cracked beneath her. She hung suspended from another, smaller branch before that broke too.

She screamed, her cry covered by thunder.

Fear gave her magic new strength. Grabbing all the wind surrounding her, she cushioned her landing. The stone pavement collided with her shoulder and side, but not hard enough to break bone. She lay there for a moment, stunned mentally as well as physically. *By All Four Gods and Goddesses, did Dorian just try to kill me? Why? He knows his season can't last forever!*

Rain returned, but Kay didn't have the will to keep herself dry. After several moments, she forced herself to get up and limp to the building door. Locked. She didn't have a key, and she didn't want to explain to the landlord what she was doing outside in her nightgown. She couldn't go back the way she had come. She'd have to hide somewhere until dawn and then sneak back inside.

Kay crossed her arms over her chest as she walked down the street. What should she do? Dorian was gone, probably back at the Season Avatar's house in Wistica. Part of her wanted to go there right now and confront Dorian. Anger carried her for a few heartbeats as she sought the closest route to the Spring Quarter. Then she halted. How could she convince Dorian's own quartet that he had tried to kill her? They'd listen to him, not her. So would anyone else, including the king, should the Four grant her a miracle that would let her come before him with a complaint.

There's no one who would believe me, except perhaps my own quartet. But I don't know where any of them are. We're probably not meant to link for years yet.

Footsteps sent Kay to hide in a shop doorway. A member of the Watch passed by in her yellow coat. Kay rested her head on the rough wall and closed her eyes.

She fell again; at least, she thought she was falling. She seemed stuck in the middle of the air as if it had turned to maple syrup. There was nothing around she could use to orient herself. She summoned the winds to rescue her, but they didn't respond. How could her magic fail her so completely? Had Winter abandoned her?

Desperate, Kay called for a cloud, rain, anything to prove her magic still existed. A small cloud formed over her head. She tried to make it grow bigger, but as she pushed magic out of herself, her hands bled. She couldn't even clench them to stop the flow. Worse, magic dripped out of her. Someone was sucking her magic right out of her soul. Kay screamed...

She found herself still in the doorway. Her hands were dry and whole, but she rubbed them together, even smelled them to make sure she wasn't bleeding. It was too dark here to tell otherwise. She knew how to make lightning balls to provide light, but she didn't dare use one.

Her dream was a warning: if she used her weather magic, she'd die.

That can't be right. I'm supposed to use my magic. Everyone in Challen depends on me to straighten out the seasons when they get mixed up. Kay stood up. *This has to be a trick Dorian is playing on me so he can continue being the Winter Avatar.* She held out her hand and prepared to summon a lightning ball. *Only...he doesn't have the magic to affect my dreams. No one does. So where did the warning come from?*

Her hand trembled. Kay couldn't will the lightning into existence.

Freeze it! If I can't use my magic, I'm useless. Useless!

She stumbled into the street, driven by the urge to get away. Away from everyone who knew her birthday was on the winter solstice. Away from everyone who would be disappointed in her. If she couldn't use her magic, she'd have to earn her living with her needle. She couldn't stay in Wistica; word would get back to her family. Besides, the Season

Avatars came to Wistica every three moons to celebrate the change of seasons. She'd have to move to another town, or even seek employment with some rich noble in a corner of Challen even the Season Avatars were unlikely to visit.

The fastest way to travel anywhere in Challen was the railroad. Kay headed toward the station, guessing more than navigating there. Fog thickened, hiding her shameful retreat. No one noticed her as she slipped into the station. She squinted at the Outbound schedule mounted on the side of a wooden shelter. She didn't have as much as a quarter-chal with her. Even if she had her reticule, she wouldn't be able to afford a trip on any of these locomotives. She'd have to sneak onboard and pray the Four concealed her.

Although no passenger trains would depart until morning, a freight train was being loaded on the far track. Kay balanced on the rails so she wouldn't make any noise on the gravel. Workmen called out to each other in voices distorted by the stillness. She crept behind a boxcar to watch them. With much complaining, they loaded crates of smoked fish, ale, and something from the country of Fip—she couldn't read the language. She waited, hoping they would move on to another car and leave this open so she could sneak inside. Instead, they filled it and shut the door. Kay tried the lock anyway. She might have been able to pick it if she had a set of needles with her, but for now, all she could do was move on.

She walked the length of the locomotive, amazed at how long it was, and tried every door she could find. Finally, she found one with a loose handle. If she could find the right tools, she could remove the handle and hide inside the boxcar.

Kay peered through the fog, which hindered her vision as little as heat or cold affected her. A long, low building squatted on the other side of the tracks. She crept closer to investigate. She kept stepping on rocks with her bare feet. All she could do was grimace and try to avoid even whispering "Freeze it." She had no idea how many workers were around or if some of them were inside that building. She would just have to take her chances.

I wish I knew if I was doing the right thing. If only Winter would give me a sign! But would He still bother to guide me since I've failed Him as an Avatar?

She folded her hands and closed her eyes. *Winter, I'm no longer worthy of being Your Avatar, but You and the rest of the Four care for everyone in Challen, Avatars or not. I can't stay in Wistica, where Dorian and that strange woman can find me. Please, if You want me to live, help me now. My life and death are in Your hands.*

She opened her eyes and watched. The fog grew thicker. Moisture beaded on her skin, but her vision remained unimpaired. Shouts and curses indicated the workers here weren't as fortunate. Was this the help she'd prayed for? If so, she'd be ungrateful not to use it.

Walking slowly so as not to make any noise, she approached the building, then circled around until she found the entrance. She watched it for several moments, afraid someone would come out and run into her. Finally, she tried the door. Unlocked, but it creaked when she pushed it open a couple of inches. Kay halted and held her breath. Still no response. She summoned her courage and entered.

Her eyes adjusted rapidly to the bright light. Inside were several long benches filled with tools she didn't recognize. She grabbed a long, thin, metal bar and turned to leave.

"You! By the Four, what are you doing here?"

An older man in a worn suit advanced on her, blocking the doorway. Kay bolted in the other direction. There had to be another exit somewhere. She passed the tables and came to an area where a partly disassembled locomotive lay spread across the floor. She hopped over wheels and pistons, outpacing the man behind her. If she could find another exit, she could hide somewhere outside, where the weather would work in her favor.

Once she cleared the train, she kept running as straight as she could. There had to be another exit on the opposite side of the building.

As she passed a shelf full of nuts and bolts, another man looked up from the bin of parts he was sorting through. This man was younger than the first one, only a few years older than Kay. He had dark hair, broad shoulders, and friendly eyes that widened when he saw her.

"Where's the nearest door?" she asked without thinking.

Still speechless, he pointed to his left.

Kay smiled to thank him and hurried in the direction he had indicated. She wondered what he would say to the man following her. Once she was back outside, she'd hide in the fog until he gave up searching for her. Then she'd creep back to the boxcar and open the door. If the train departed before she could sneak on, she'd choose another one. Anything to leave Wistica and find safety.

Kay ran past a little sitting area around a pipe stove. Half-full cups of chocolate and plates of toast tempted her to grab a bite. Magic always made her so hungry…but she wouldn't need to worry about that ever again. With a sob, she continued to the door. She opened it and stepped out into the clear night.

Where did the fog go? How am I supposed to hide?

As if being exposed wasn't bad enough, she was in a different part of the train yard and wasn't sure how to retrace her steps. If she ran around to the other side of the building, she'd probably get caught. If only she could use her magic—or dared to. She wasn't desperate enough for that yet.

Kay studied her surroundings. Rows of boxcars and passenger cars—she could tell them apart by the fancy trim and windows on the latter—lined up on short stretches of track. No locomotives were visible. She guessed this must be a holding area for train cars not in use. No sense breaking into one of these. However, there had to be track she could follow to the main line. After some searching, she found it. She also found the young man who'd directed her to the door. He carried an extra coat with him, and as soon as he spotted her, he hurried toward her. She glanced at the train cars flanking her. Both of them were closed. Even if they had been open, she'd have only trapped herself by fleeing into one.

"Wait!" the man called. His voice was just loud enough to carry to her. "Who are you? What are you doing here?"

Kay hesitated, unsure what to tell him.

He approached her, holding the coat in front of him like an offering to the Four. "Here. You must be wet and cold."

"I'm not—" She bit her lip. Any normal young woman caught out in the rain would be miserable. Besides, if she wandered around wearing nothing more than her nightgown, someone would think she was a lightskirt. "I mean, thank you."

She allowed him to slip the coat over her shoulders. The bottom hem hung below her knees, and her arms swum in the sleeves. At least she felt more decent.

"I'm Jon Stunstrug, a fireman. Who are you? Are you trying to go somewhere? We don't have any passenger trains leaving until dawn."

Kay swallowed. "I'm Kay Seltich." She hoped he didn't know the next generation of Season Avatars. "I'm a seamstress. I need to leave Wistica before they kill me."

Mr. Stunstrug's eyes widened again. They were as brown and warm as a cup of chocolate. "What? By All Four Gods and Goddesses, who would want to kill you?"

"I can't explain." She wished she could. Anyone with such an open expression had to be trustworthy. "But the ones who are after me…they're powerful. Very powerful. I can't let them find me."

The fireman frowned slightly. Worrying he didn't believe her, she added, "I swear it by the Four, especially Winter."

He smiled at that. "I'm Winterborn too. Not many people claim Him as their favorite God." He took her hands in his calloused ones and rubbed them. Thrills as intense as lightning jolted up her arms. She repressed a gasp.

Mr. Stunstrug pulled away, leaving her flesh feeling bereft. "Forgive me, Dama, I thought you'd be cold. Winter must have treated you more gently than I expected."

"No, no, you didn't have to stop! I mean, I'm well." Her cheeks grew warm. Even in previous lives, when she'd had to speak at a soltrans, her tongue always tied itself too easily.

He stared at her for a couple of heartbeats, making her blush more furiously, before asking, "Where were you planning to go?"

"I don't know. Somewhere I can earn a living with a needle. Only…I don't even have a needle with me." It came to her how foolish this was, trying to flee the city without a quarter-chal, a reticule, shoes, or a spare change of clothes. All she had was a magical gift she didn't dare use and enough strength to keep her fears and frustration squeezed inside.

"I…I have an idea." Mr. Stunstrug glanced about before putting his hands on her shoulders and leaning forward. "There's a town in north-western Challen called Rainbow River. It's good sheep country out there, so they dye, spin, and weave wool. I'm sure you could find some-one there who could use a seamstress."

Kay nodded. With so many other seamstresses about, Dorian and the strange woman would never be able to find her as long as she didn't use her magic. "It sounds wonderful. Only…it must be so far away!"

"There's a freight train headed there tonight, as soon as they finish loading coal and water. There are no passenger cars, but if you were willing to hide in a boxcar for a couple of days, it would take you there." Mr. Stunstrug swallowed. "Mind you, I could lose my job for this if I'm caught."

"I'll be very quiet," she said. "No one will ever notice me."

"I find it hard to believe no one would ever notice a pretty dama like you."

He thinks I'm pretty? Kay glanced down at herself to see if her body was still stick-thin. The barest trace of womanly curves were just be-ginning to show. Her dark hair didn't extend past her chin, and her skin was so pale strangers often thought she was ill. He had to be flattering her, but she couldn't help liking it.

As she struggled to find a response, the first man shouted, "Jon, where are you? I need your help!"

Kay tensed. She tried the door of the nearest boxcar, but it was locked.

"These cars can't move," Mr. Stunstrug whispered. "If you can crawl under one, he'll never find you. Wait here until I return."

"But your coat will get dirty."

He smiled. "I spend most of my time shoveling coal, Dama. I'm the one who should apologize for getting you dirty."

"Jon!"

"I'm coming!" he shouted back. He gestured for her to hide. This time, she slipped under the boxcar, wincing as she crunched gravel. Mr. Stunstrug hurried off.

Kay flattened herself against the stones. Mr. Stunstrug's coat offered some protection, but they still pressed against her skin. She wrapped herself as best as she could in the coat for camouflage. Footsteps echoed in the distance. If she dared use her magic, she could have the wind carry other sounds to her. She could eavesdrop on Mr. Stunstrug and the older man who might be his supervisor. Would Mr. Stunstrug tell him about her? She couldn't imagine a man with such soulful eyes and strong hands could betray her. Then again, she'd never thought Dorian would attempt to eliminate her before she'd even become a Season Avatar. Kay sighed. She couldn't trust anyone, could she?

I wish I knew who the other Season Avatars in my quartet are. I could go to one of them for help. She knew all birth records were kept in the Hall of Records in Wistica, in the Spring Quarter. Would anyone there be willing to help her? In her bare feet and borrowed coat, she didn't look like an Avatar. The record-keepers might contact the current Season Avatars to identify her, and that would bring her to Dorian's attention. She couldn't even go to the Temple for fear of running into him. The only way she could assure her safety was to go somewhere the Season Avatars would never visit and no one knew her name. Rainbow River would do. Even if Mr. Stunstrug remembered her later, she'd have blended in with the other workers before then.

Kay allowed herself a final sigh and hugged the coat tightly. She shouldn't keep it, even if it reminded her of him. Perhaps she could abandon it somewhere where he could find it. At least she hadn't lost the strip of metal she'd risked everything to find.

She couldn't hear footsteps anymore, but she waited a few more heartbeats before poking her head out of her hiding place. When nothing happened, she crept out and dropped the coat next to the boxcar. She pressed herself against the train cars as she crept out into the open. Kay waited several heartbeats. Sticking to shadows as much as possible, she headed back the way she had come. Part of her hoped she'd encounter Mr. Stunstrug again, but she didn't hear or see him anywhere. Maybe his supervisor had called him away for some other reason than to look for her. Maybe she would be safe…

The wind shifted, turning colder. Too cold. *Chaos Season.* Freeze it, was the magic weather storm a coincidence, or Dorian trying to find her? She hurried. No one would hear her footsteps with the wind making noise. Maybe this storm would help her instead of hindering her. Snow drifted down, becoming thicker with each passing heartbeat. If it grew too thick, even she would have trouble seeing through it. Would the locomotives be able to travel? Chaos Season shouldn't last very long, but it could cause a lot of problems before the Season Avatars tamed it.

If only I dared tame this storm myself. Chaos Season was so powerful it took four Avatars to control it, but the Winter Avatar was the only one who could tap the storm's magic directly. She could do it; she'd done it in previous lives. She just didn't dare. Dorian would sense her interference. Kay didn't know what the other woman would do to her, but it wouldn't be good.

Snow built up as she shuffled forward. She strained to see through the blizzard. Something dark moved in front of her. Mr. Stunstrug? He didn't seem to notice her. He was facing away from her, saying something to the other man.

The snow turned into freezing rain. Kay could have shielded herself from getting wet, but she allowed the rain to sluice her hair and nightgown. Her feet automatically resisted getting cut by the ice or frostbitten by the snow. The men, however, had no such protection.

Freeze it, I can't let them suffer! Centuries of instinct built up by previous lives took over. Kay tapped into the storm itself. As its power weakened in their immediate area, she warmed the air. The snow and ice melted. Visibility improved as the precipitation faded away. Mr. Stunstrug turned and smiled at her.

Before she could say anything to him, she felt electricity build in the air, right over her. *Dorian knows I'm here!* She grabbed the lightning and diverted it to strike a nearby metal building. Then she released her connection to the weather and ran past the men. She thought she heard Mr. Stunstrug calling "Dama!" The air shimmered with unexpected heat of summer. As snow melted, Kay struggled for footing. A cry sounded behind her, but she didn't look to see what had happened.

The locomotives she'd seen before finally reappeared. Kay dove into the first open boxcar she found. She squeezed between crates of smoked fish. Her stomach rumbled. She pried a crate corner open with the metal strip, then devoured chunks of fish. They left her thirsty, but they restored the energy she'd burned by using magic.

By the Four, it didn't take Dorian long to find me once I used magic. The wind picked up and rattled the boxcar as if trying to shake her out. Kay held her breath. *I'm not here. I'm not here. I'm not the one you're seeking....*

The wind finally died. It felt like ages passed before someone slammed the boxcar door shut. Despite the perfect darkness, Kay didn't conjure up a lightning ball, as she would have normally done. She might have survived using magic, but it drew her enemies to her.

Eventually, a whistle sounded far away. The boxcar began to move, slowly at first, then picking up speed. She was committed to this course now. Had she made the right decision?

God of Winter, forgive me if I hold off on serving You now. I can't be part of my quartet if Dorian sends me to Your domain of the dead. Forgive me, but it's not the right season yet for my magic. She stared as light gleamed through a crack in the wall. *Someday the season will change. I just have to live long enough to see it.*

To Name the Anilink

Ysabel glanced up and down the hallway, making sure her sister Bethany wasn't spying on her. Father always insisted Selathen maidens shouldn't leave the house without a chaperone. He didn't trust that the Goddess of Fall would protect all women in the country no matter what their background was. Ysabel knew better. She was Fall's Avatar, charged with protecting all the animals in Challen, and right now a mother cat was giving birth in the stable where Father kept his horse. Ysabel didn't think the mother was in danger, but the cat wordlessly pled for her to come. She couldn't deny the creature, no matter what her father thought.

She detoured through the kitchen, both to avoid detection by her younger siblings and to beg some scraps from the cook. Lathtin had always been better at wheedling food, but he couldn't help her now. As much as she loved animals, he had loved medicine—the herbal and surgery kind, not the magical healing practiced by the Spring Avatar. Unfortunately, Lathtin hadn't shared the Spring Avatar's natural immunity to disease. He'd succumbed to illness during an outbreak last year. Ever since then, Papa had become even sterner, Mama had withdrawn, and Ysabel's siblings had grown even more unruly. Two governesses and the nursemaid had given notice, leaving Ysabel minding the children and taking time away from her true calling. Thank the Four the youngest children were napping—or supposed to be napping. Now all Ysabel had to do was avoid Bethany—

"Where are you going, sister?" Bethany asked, blocking the hallway. She held an apple, so she must have been in the kitchen. Maybe it was a good thing they'd encountered each other here.

"Looking for something to tide me over until dinner," Ysabel said, putting on a smile. "What's Cook willing to part with?"

"For you? Chicken gizzards." Bethany smirked. "I hope you eat them yourself instead of giving them to your flea-ridden pests."

Ysabel had to restrain herself from saying her animals didn't have fleas. She could drive them away, along with bed bugs and other pests. Although she kept the insects out of her room and Mama's, she had to allow them in other parts of the house, in case someone wondered why the Lathatilltins were so blessed.

She squared her shoulders. "I haven't brought home any animals in moons." Not since Lathtin had gone to the God of Winter and could help her hide them—or, at worst, claim they were his, not hers. Fall Avatars were always women, so no one would suspect him of having animal magic.

"Good. Keep it that way. I don't want them damaging my dresses." Bethany spun around, showing off how she'd altered Ysabel's hand-me-down with more ribbons and lace than Ysabel had in her entire wardrobe.

Looking at the dress gave Ysabel an idea. "Bethany," she said slowly, as if she might reconsider, "My pearl gray gloves are too small on me, but they might fit you—"

"I'll try them on. They would suit this outfit perfectly." Bethany raced upstairs before Ysabel could change her mind. For her part, Ysabel hurried to the kitchen. Sacrificing a pair of gloves would be worth it if she could make it to the stable without more interference from Bethany.

The kitchen smelled of garlic and lemon. Fish heads sat in a pail by the sink. Cook hulled berries for a cobbler while the maid-of-all-work scrubbed a pot. "Afternoon, Dama," Cook said. "Looking for something for yourself—or a friend?"

"A friend," Ysabel replied. She peered at the fish heads and decided against bringing them. "No meat scraps today?"

"I'm afraid not, Dama."

She repressed a sigh. Food for the pregnant cat would have been nice, but Ysabel could feel her going into labor. There wasn't time to find anything else if Ysabel wanted to be there when the kittens arrived. "That's all right, then." She edged toward the back door to the kitchen garden. "I'll just…take some fresh air."

As she left, she heard Cook chuckle. Thank the Four her father would never think of asking his staff where his children were. As long as she made sure he didn't see her at the stable, she would be fine.

Ysabel hurried to the back gate and passed through it into an alley scarcely wide enough for a pair of horses. She dodged around steaming piles of manure and rotting kitchen waste. Once she reached the main street, she encountered more people, mostly servants busy on their own errands. A gang of urchins taunted her, but they followed her at a distance, careful not to get too close or annoy her too much. She'd encountered them before and had set rats on them.

She slipped inside the stable while the owner was busy scolding a stable boy about poorly cleaned harnesses. The owner knew Ysabel could calm horses, but he seemed more uncomfortable with her every time she visited. Most Selathen young women her age wouldn't haunt a public stable no matter how much they loved horses. Selathen men wouldn't employ women, who were supposed to stay home and raise children. Ysabel hoped to have her own brood someday—hopefully better behaved than her siblings—but they wouldn't be allowed to interfere with her work as a Fall Avatar. She would be responsible not just for the welfare of all animals in Challen, but also helping the other three Season Avatars tame Chaos Season, the magical weather storm that mixed up the seasons. Challen were more accommodating of women's rights than Selathens were, even though Selathens had been living in Challen for centuries. Life would be easier once Ysabel was recognized as the next Fall Avatar and could move to the One Oak, the Season Avatars' traditional home in the center of the country.

How will that happen if no one knows my true birthday is the first day of fall, not the last day of summer? Mama says she didn't even dare to put the correct date on my birth record, in case Papa saw it before she sent it to the Hall of Records in Wistica. But how will the other Avatars ever find me if they don't know I'm the one they're looking for? Ysabel sighed. *Maybe I'll have to make my own way to the One Oak when I'm needed. A Spring Avatar will be able to tell who I am by looking at my aura. Of course, I'll have to demonstrate my magic too. It would be nice to have an anilink by then.*

Like Summer Avatars with their oak trees, Fall Avatars bonded with a special animal that helped boost their magic. Anilinks could also sense when a Chaos Season started anywhere in Challen and warn their Avatars. Best of all, anilinks were smarter than other animals of their kind and could communicate with their partners mentally. Having an anilink meant that Ysabel would never be lonely in a household of people that didn't know her secret.

The mother cat yowled, reminding Ysabel why she'd come. She scurried to the back of the stable where the feed was kept. The mother cat, mostly black except for white paws, had made a nest for herself between bales of hay. Ysabel squeezed in next to her. Stalks of hay poked through her clothes and made her itch. Although Ysabel hadn't met this particular cat before, the mother cat purred as she sniffed Ysabel. Animals always knew she could help them. The cat lay on her side, licking her belly and beneath her tail. The birth seemed to be proceeding normally, so Ysabel sat back and watched.

Time passed as horses were saddled, harnessed, unharnessed, and groomed. Ysabel watched the light change through the narrow window and wondered how much longer she had until she would be missed at home. The cat shifted into a squatting position, so Ysabel touched her to ease her labor.

A few moments later, the first kitten sac slid out. The mama licked the kitten's mouth, tearing the sac. The kitten, a female, took her first breath. As soon as the mama bit the cord through, the kitten stumbled to her mama's side to begin nursing. Two more kittens arrived without any problems.

Ysabel sensed a fourth one wedged in the birth canal. A gentle pressing with her fingertips and a small release of magic solved the problem. Ysabel used more magic to hasten the kitten's passage. He popped out in a couple of heartbeats. The mama cat was too busy cleaning up the afterbirths from the previous kittens to lick him. He tilted his head, eyes squeezed tightly closed, toward Ysabel, not his mother.

Ysabel held her breath. A very faint mew sounded in her mind. None of the other kittens had paid her any attention. Could this be her anilink? She searched her memories of previous lives for her initial meetings with her other anilinks. Many of her prior anilinks had been wild animals that she'd encountered when they'd been injured. Some of them had been infants, but she'd never bonded with an anilink when it was a newborn.

Hello there, little one, she thought at him. *I'm Ysabel.* If he was destined to be her anilink, he would be able to hear her, even if he was too young to understand. Would he respond? If so, how?

The kitten mewed in her head again, louder this time. *Isa?*

He formed a human word, and he was barely four minutes old! He had to be her anilink. Ysabel wanted to squeeze him and take him home, but he was too delicate for that yet.

He struggled toward her, still encased in his birth sac. Worried he wouldn't get enough air, Ysabel tore the sac open herself. She rubbed his wet fur very gently with an underskirt, amazed at how tiny yet perfectly formed he was. Like his mother, he was mostly black, but he had white markings on his chest and other places.

"You need a name," she told him. "But what?" Coloration offered obvious choices, but she didn't want to use anything with black or white or spots. Maybe she should wait until he got a little older and started displaying more personality. For now, she gently pushed him back toward his mother so he could nurse. "You're not ready to come home with me," she said. "You have to be at least two moons old first."

"Dama Lathatilltin? Who are you talking to?"

She turned her head to find a stable boy watching her. "No one," she said hastily, resisting the urge to sweep hay over the cats.

"Well, you'd better hurry before your father arrives. He's coming down the street now."

Freeze it! She rose and brushed hay off of her clothes. "Thank you for the warning."

She reached out to her father's gelding and suggested he take objection to a flock of starlings—not seriously enough to unseat her father, but enough to delay him for a few minutes so she could sneak out of the stable. Unfortunately, her father wasn't the only customer who recognized her.

"Disobedient wench, get home where you belong!" a man shouted at her. "You shame your family!"

What a freezing foolish attitude, she thought. *What harm is there in newborn kittens, especially one that might be mine? I hope the mother bonds with him enough to nurse him properly. If he's meant to be my anilink, he needs to grow big and strong. How soon will I be able to go back and visit him?*

***

Ysabel's trip to the stable didn't go unnoticed. Either her sister had figured out where she had gone, or else someone at the stable had given her away. Perhaps her father had seen her fleeing despite her delaying tactic. Whatever had happened, she was summoned into his private office, which reeked of smoke from his pipe. There he gave her a stern lecture and forbade her from leaving the house at all for at least a quarter-moon. Even Cook obeyed his order and refused to let her step into the garden. All Ysabel could do was stare out of her bedroom window toward the stable and extend her magic as far as possible, trying to reach her anilink. It seemed impossible she'd be able to make contact with such a young mind, and for several days she heard nothing from him. She constantly fretted something would happen to the kitten. Perhaps his mother would refuse to let him nurse, or one of the horses in the stable would accidentally step on him.

If only Lathtin were still alive. I wouldn't trust anyone else to check on my kitten.

Finally, the day before her punishment would end, her mental calls received a response. *Ysbel?* The thought that followed wasn't words as much as feelings and sensory images. She felt fear and abandonment as the kitten searched in vain for her scent and her touch.

I'm here, she told him over and over again. *I'll be there soon.*

How could she manage that when everyone in the household would be watching her? She wouldn't be surprised if her father had arranged with the stable owner to have her turned away.

Ysabel reached under her bed for a small jewelry box. Although she kept it locked, it didn't contain gems or gold. Instead, she used it to store the most perfect autumn leaves she could find, in every shade of red, yellow, and brown. Just smelling them made her smile and think of fall, her true birth season.

Goddess of Fall, I don't understand yet why you chose this family to raise me until I can serve You as the next Fall Avatar, but I trust You have a reason. How can I see my possible anilink again when my movements are so restricted? She sighed. *Have You ever had to deal with men who didn't respect women properly? Why can't You teach these Selathens a lesson? Not all of them, just the ones who won't let women do the same things men can. Lathtin gave You Your proper due—*

Ysabel halted her prayer. The Goddess had just given her the answer. It might not help her leave the house, but it should help her reach the stable undetected. If she planned properly, she might even be able to make regular visits to her kitten until the day he was old enough to come home.

***

The next day, while the governess struggled to teach the younger children how to spell their names, Ysabel snuck into Lathtin's room. The maid-of-all-work still cleaned it as if he would return. The room smelled of cedar and lemon wax polish. Lathtin's rock and insect collections cluttered his desk. Ysabel shut the door behind her and stood against it for a few heartbeats, remembering other times when she and her twin brother had snuck into each other's room at night. When they were five or six, they'd found it easier to face the scary night together instead of in separate beds. They'd only stopped doing it when Lathtin's tutor had caned him twice: once for her and once for him. She smiled wryly. If Lathtin had been willing to endure that, he wouldn't object to her borrowing his clothes to pass herself off as a boy.

His clothes had been neatly folded in a chest at the foot of the bed. Ysabel held up a pair of brown pants and a tan tunic, clothes Lathtin had worn to ride or sneak out to meet his friends for misadventures. They still smelled of him. Maybe that would help her fool people into thinking she was a boy. She couldn't cut her hair—it would raise too many questions—so she needed all the help she could get. She held the clothes up to herself. The sleeves and pants were too long, but she could hem them herself. She rummaged around in the chest until she found a cap to hide her hair. That should be enough for her disguise. She left Lathtin's room—and ran into Bethany.

"What are you doing with those?" Ysabel's sister asked.

"I'm going to make them over." It was the first answer that came to Ysabel.

"For what?"

"Well, it's a waste having them sit there, isn't it?" She made a show of checking the width of the pants. "I could turn them into a skirt if I could find matching material. Or I could cut them down for the boys."

Bethany shrugged. "Too plain for a skirt. Give it to Tal."

"I don't suppose you want to help..." Ysabel let the sentence trail off, as if she didn't care either way.

"I have enough to do keeping my own wardrobe presentable. Father doesn't give us anywhere near enough of a clothing allowance to keep us in proper fashion. How will we make brilliant matches if we don't attend the best balls?"

"It's too soon to worry about that. Lathtin went to the God of Winter only six moons ago."

"You could be out if you chose." Bethany glared at her. "Why aren't you trying to attract suitors? You're of age to wed, and Father won't allow me to marry until you're settled."

Bethany was only thirteen, so she was several years away from being out. As for Ysabel, Mama insisted she couldn't marry because she was needed at home. That was what she told Father; Ysabel knew it was to keep her as free as possible until she was ready to join the other Season Avatars in her quartet and live at the One Oak.

Ysabel put on a smile. "We'll see who offers for me." She escaped to her room before Bethany could question her further.

It took Ysabel several days to alter the clothes in secret. Her time of confinement ended. She waited until laundry day, when the servants were busy, and offered to run a few errands for the cook. No one questioned her as she left with a basket. Hidden under a towel were Lathtin's altered clothes. She scurried down the alley until she found a hidden nook to change in, drawing Lathtin's old pants up under her skirt before removing the outer garment. Every heartbeat she expected someone to catch her, even though the rats in the alley assured her no one was coming. Ysabel couldn't help smiling as she tucked her hair under the cap. This might be the closest she would ever come to living as a male, so she planned to experience as much of it as she could.

Ysabel attempted to stride the way Lathtin always had, with long steps that had forced her to run to keep up. She kept the basket close to her chest and folded her arms over it, both to hide her bosom and to keep others from remembering the basket later, when she ran errands as herself.

She approached the stable from the back way. She hid the basket next to some bags of grain and asked a pair of pigeons to watch over it. *May the Four watch over me.* She put on a hopeful expression as she approached the stable owner. "Need someone to muck out the stable?" She tried to deepen her voice, but it quavered at the end.

The stable owner scowled and leaned closer to her as if he could penetrate her disguise. She could smell tobacco on his breath. "Who are you? You look familiar."

She swallowed, trying to keep the name of her older brother from escaping. He would realize Lathtin was the name of the Honored Lathatilltin's oldest and absent son. Hopefully Ysabel's father had never bothered to mention how many children he had or what their names were.

"Tal, sir."

"Tal, heh?" He rubbed his chin. "And how long have you been in Traderstown?

"All my life, sir. My family's come on hard times, so I want to help out."

"You don't look like you're starving, but fine." He gestured back toward the stable. "A half chal when you're done, if you do a good job."

Ysabel smiled and nodded, fighting down her panic. Freeze it, would she have to follow through with the chore? All she wanted to do was visit her kitten. Maybe she'd be able to figure out what his name should be.

She sent quick greetings to the horses as she passed, but she headed straight to the back room, pretending she didn't see shovels and pitchforks in an empty stall. The mother cat laid her ears flat and hissed at Ysabel when she prodded at the nest, but the cat calmed down as Ysabel sent her reassurance.

"By the Four, your babies are growing faster than weeds," Ysabel murmured. They were already twice as big as they'd been at birth, and their eyes were open. The entire litter stumbled toward her. For a moment, she wondered if she'd imagined one of them seeking her out at birth. Then the black-and-white male—still smaller than the others, she noted—lifted his head toward her, nostrils flaring. A spark of joy not her own flared in her mind.

"You are my anilink!" She inspected each of the other kittens quickly before picking up the one she considered her own. He rumbled, though he was too young for a real purr.

"What would be a good name for you?" She gently touched a finger to the top of his head. She had the feeling—too subtle to tell if it came from him or not—that he should have a name inspired by his behavior, not his appearance.

The owner poked his head in the room. "Hey, Tal! What are you doing back here? Get to work! If you're stealing anything—"

Ysabel hastily set the kitten down next to his mother, but the stable owner came over to her and directed his scowl downward. "Ugh, another litter! I should drown them now!"

"No, don't!" In her panic, Ysabel forgot to lower her voice.

The owner peered at her face. "What did you say, boy—if that's what you are?" He frowned. "Who are you really?"

The animals around Ysabel caught her fear. Horses nickered and stamped in their stalls, and the mother cat flattened her ears and hissed.

The stable owner swore. "Come help me with the horses, and then we'll talk." He dashed out to the main part of the barn.

Ysabel didn't follow. Even if the owner changed his mind about drowning the litter, this place was too dangerous for her anilink. If the owner had penetrated her disguise, she wouldn't be able to return here. Worse, if the owner told her father she'd been here after having been forbidden to visit, not only would she get in trouble again, but her father would try to investigate why she kept returning. She couldn't let him suspect the animals drew her.

Flee! She told the mother cat. *Take your babies!* This cat wouldn't be able to understand her language, but she would sense the fear and urgency in her thoughts.

The mama immediately grabbed her oldest kitten by the scruff of the neck and bounded off. The kitten squeaked like a rat.

Safety here. Ysabel projected an image of an abandoned rabbit hole by the back entrance of her family's house. She scooped up her anilink and his siblings, wishing she'd brought the basket in with her so she could carry them easier. They'd grown so much they spilled over her hands. The kittens protested with soft mews, but her anilink laid his head trustingly on her arm. Hopefully he would inspire his siblings to behave.

Ysabel dashed into the stable. The horses were still restless and refused to let the stable owner or any of the other employees lay hands on them. "Hey!" the owner shouted at her. "I thought you were going to help us!"

Wait until I leave the stable yard, she sent to the horses.

The stable hands clogged the narrow passage between the stalls, but they gave her space to pass. She edged as far away from the owner as she could, but he grabbed her arm. "Who are you?" He peered closer at her face. "What are you?"

Ysabel didn't know what would be worse: him learning her name or that she was the next Fall Avatar. She tried pulling against his grip, but he was stronger than her. The horses were already agitated but confined to their stalls, her anilink too young and helpless to defend her—what else could Ysabel do?

Words from another life came back to her: *Sometimes the smallest animals can have bigger impacts than anyone realizes.*

She scanned the stable for pests she could turn against the owner. She'd done him a favor by ridding all his horses of parasites, and the mama cat had taken care of the mice and rats. Ysabel had left the spiders alone, since they were harmless and ate insects. Now she summoned them down on their silken threads, making them think the stable owner was a tasty meal. They congregated on him in heartbeats.

"Look at all those spiders!" A stable hand pointed at a dozen of them.

The stable owners shook his head, trying to dislodge them. They crept under his hat and into his ears. With a shriek, he released Ysabel to swat at the spiders. She ran, instructing the spiders to flee as well before they were killed.

Once she left the stable yard, she headed straight home, since the mama cat was well ahead of her. Halfway there, Ysabel remembered she'd left her original clothing and the basket behind. She sighed. When Father found out, she'd get into more trouble. She prayed to the Four that Bethany would be somewhere else so she wouldn't witness Ysabel's return home.

By the time she reached the back gate, her arms ached with the effort of trying to hold three squirming kittens without dropping any. She managed to free a hand to work the latch, then knelt next to the rabbit hole to reunite the kittens with their mother. The hole was still empty. Alarmed, Ysabel stood, allowing the kittens to explore the strange grass, and searched for the mother cat. Had she been delayed with her other kitten, gotten lost, or perhaps hurt? None of her worries had come true; the cat had stubbornly decided to pick a different nest closer to the house. She'd found a spot next to the kitchen, where the stove gave off warmth and the mama cat could find scraps. In many ways it was a better place than the one Ysabel had suggested, though the cook or girl-of-all-work was more likely to discover the litter. Hopefully they wouldn't react the same way as the stable owner.

Ysabel brought the squirming kittens over to their mother. The two normal ones started nursing, but her anilink clung to her. *I won't be far,* she reassured him as she gently removed his tiny claws from her sleeve.

Once she persuaded him to stay with his family, she stood on tiptoe to peer in the kitchen window. The cook prepared a chicken while the girl-of-all-work boiled sheets in front of the fire. Ysabel wondered if she could retrieve her own clothes and the basket, then run the errand as she was supposed to. When she returned to the nook, her belongings were gone. Freeze it, she should have recruited a creature to watch them for her. Thank the Four she still had the money. Ysabel ran the errands as a boy, speaking as little as possible and in a gruff voice. She didn't have enough money to replace the basket, so she struggled not to drop her load on the way home. At least vegetables didn't squirm and claw her. She dropped her load on the back porch. *There.* Now to sneak into the house before someone saw her.

Ysabel studied the upstairs windows and wondered if she could climb up to them. There weren't any trees close enough to the house. Besides, all the windows were shut from the inside.

Lathtin, where are you when I need you? You could lower a sheet ladder and pull me up, or draw their attention. Of course, if you were here, you would have helped me get to the stable or found some way to bring my anilink to me. Brother, I hope the God of Winter is feasting you well. Will you be reborn into my life again?

She wiped her face with her sleeve. Lathtin would tell her to stop sniveling and get on with it. Well, then, the easiest way into the house was through the kitchen. Should she hope the servants were too busy with their tasks to notice her, or try to distract them first?

I'd better distract them, just to make sure. Ysabel probed to see what other animals were around. Mice would have been ideal for causing a commotion, but she didn't allow rodents in the house. The mother cat was nursing, so Ysabel couldn't ask her to make a scene.

If I don't have any real animals to help me, I'll have to do it myself. Maybe an animal call? Lathtin had been better at imitating birds and other animals, but after so many lives as the Fall Avatar, Ysabel knew all the sounds animals could make. She thought for a moment, then crept under the kitchen window and imitated the high-pitched squealing of a bat. She pressed up close against the house to listen. No change. She squealed again, loud enough to make the mother cat look at her with a surprised expression.

The cook said, "Did you hear that, Hanna?"

"Hear what, Dame?"

Ysabel squealed a third time, shifting over so they would think the bat was trapped in the cupboard."

"I thought I heard something that time, Dame, but it's pretty faint."

"Never mind." Dishes rattled. "I'm sure Dama Ysabel will take care of it when she returns. She should have been born in fall, not summer, since she has the Goddess's own touch with animals. Whatever is keeping her? I can't roast this chicken until I have lemons and shallots."

Freeze it, this wasn't going to work either. Ysabel couldn't think of another trick to distract the servants—at least, nothing that wouldn't cause more trouble than it solved. Maybe the easiest solution would be to dash through the house and hope no one saw her.

She gathered her purchases, took a deep breath, and fumbled with the kitchen door until she opened it. The cook turned her head to look at her.

"Dama! There you are!" Cook raised her eyebrows. "Child, what happened to you?"

Ysabel felt her cheeks grow warm. She dropped the supplies, hoping they would keep Cook and Hanna busy, and fled up the back staircase. They only had two servants, so it would be unoccupied. She could slip into her room and change before anyone else noticed what she was wearing…

Bethany, arms crossed, leaned against the door to Ysabel's room. Ysabel skidded to a stop, nearly tripping as the rug in the hallway slid on the floorboards.

"Well, well, well, what are you wearing, Ysabel?" Bethany smirked. "Are those Lathtin's clothes?"

"You'll have to get your own."

Bethany sniffed. "As if I would be caught dead wearing men's clothing." Her voice took on a gloating tone. "And you'll wish you were dead when Father finds out."

Oh, By the Four....at least Bethany didn't know about the mother cat and her kittens...yet. Best to keep her distracted and let her think she'd won something over Ysabel.

"You wouldn't tell him, would you?" Ysabel grasped her sister's arm and put on a pleading expression.

"Maybe not...if you let me have that pearl necklace Mama gave you for your sixteenth birthday."

Ysabel couldn't help grimacing. Pearls were a tribute to the Goddess of Fall. They were also reserved for women of marriageable age. Bethany might be starting to notice men, especially well-dressed ones, but she was still too young for the necklace or what it meant.

"You can borrow it," she said, hoping that would be enough to satisfy Bethany.

Her sister shook her head. "No, I want it. Now."

"All right." Ysabel reached for the door again, relieved when Bethany allowed her to enter. "But you'd better not tell Father."

If you do, I'll send spiders to spin webs over your face while you sleep. I'm sure your breath would help them catch more flies than they can eat.

Bethany followed her into the tiny room. Ysabel unlocked her jewelry box and stared at the pearl necklace for a couple of heartbeats before handing it over. "Please take good care of it."

"It's mine now, and I can do whatever I want with it." She draped them over her neck and preened in front of Ysabel's mirror.

"Then By the Four, get out of here!"

Once Ysabel finally had privacy, she changed back into a plain gray dress. She didn't want to draw attention to herself at dinner tonight. She hoped Bethany wouldn't be foolish enough to wear the pearls. If her parents noticed them and started asking questions, Bethany might reveal Ysabel's secret, intentionally or not. And if Papa investigated, he might find Ysabel's anilink and kill him.

* * *

The next moon and a half was torture for Ysabel. Despite having gotten her way with the necklace, Bethany still threatened to tattle on Ysabel, forcing her to give up more jewelry, lace and ribbons, a fan, and even a favorite dress, which Bethany proceeded to have made over as gaudily as possible. Ysabel cringed at the result, but she said nothing. There had to be a way to get back at her sister, or spin the season around and learn something damaging about Bethany that would give Ysabel a counter-threat. Normally Ysabel wouldn't consider doing something like that to her sister, but she didn't want to lose all of her belongings before she was summoned to the One Oak. It couldn't be much longer if Fall had gifted her with her anilink, but Ysabel needed to protect him. Once Bethany noticed the kittens, she'd report them to Father, and he would have no more tolerance for them than the stable owner had.

Ysabel spent her time helping her mother and the servants around the house, practicing the pianoforte, and being the best model of a young Selathen maiden she could. Cook took her aside one morning while Hanna was cleaning upstairs and Ysabel was shelling peas.

"Dama Ysabel, I don't mean to stick my nose where it don't belong, but things have been strange around here recently, haven't they? I don't know why you were wearing that mannish outfit last moon or what happened to our basket—"

Ysabel's cheeks grew warm. "I'm sorry about that. I can buy you another one."

"Don't worry about that, Dama. It was worn, and your mother already gave us leave to purchase another. But does it have anything to do with the strange noises I hear in the garden? It sounds like there are some animals—maybe cats—in the garden."

"They're not doing any harm," Ysabel said quickly.

"I'm surprised to hear you say that, Dama. I found carcasses of songbirds when I brought the scraps outside to the garden, and something's digging through the scrap heap and the trash."

"The mama cat just needs to feed her kittens for another moon or so, and then they'll leave. Well, most of them."

Cook sighed. "Don't tell me you plan to keep one as a pet."

How could she explain her need for an anilink when no one was supposed to know she had animal magic? Maybe it was better to let the cook think it was a pet. Ysabel nodded and dumped the shelled peas into another bowl. "Don't worry. I'll take care of him myself."

Cook brought over a pile of onions. "Could you chop these up, Dama? I'm sure your father wouldn't approve. A cat will scratch all the furniture and leave hair and bad odors all over the house. I should think a young lady of your age would be ready for a husband and children of your own."

"I'll always have time for animals." Ysabel sniffed, trying not to water the onions.

Cook watched her for a few moments before saying, "I've seen you take half your lunch and give it to the birds, even when you've barely eaten yourself. You do have a way with creatures only an Ava Fall could have."

"But I was born during summer, not fall." Ysabel recited the old lie as easily as if it were the truth.

"A pity." Cook eyed her for a few heartbeats before pulling eggs out of the icebox. "I suppose I should start ordering bigger cuts of meat to make sure you get enough to eat. A husband's going to want more curves on you, Dama."

A husband couldn't be allowed to interfere with her calling as the next Fall Avatar. Ysabel planned to protest if Father tried to match her to a local Selathen man. They tended not to worship the Four and, according to Mother, didn't give women the respect they received in the rest of Challen. But if Cook was willing to help Ysabel with more food for her and the cats, it would be a blessing. Food never stretched far enough when Ysabel was performing magic.

"Thank you." She smiled despite her burning eyes.

"Just keep your pet away from your sister if you don't want her to take it too."

"I'll keep a close eye on him," Ysabel vowed. *And several on my sister. If I can persuade the cats or the birds to spy on her, I can figure out how to put an end to her blackmailing ways.*

* * *

As often was the case when managing the animals of Challen, Ysabel was caught between the needs of two different types of animals. Ever since the cat family had moved onto the property, the songbirds—at least those intelligent or healthy enough to avoid the mother cat—had stopped coming to visit Ysabel. She missed their cheerful voices and constant activity. They would make excellent spies, as they could perch in a tree near Bethany's window, and she'd never notice them. But even if Ysabel could override the birds' instincts for self-preservation, how could she prevent the mother cat from stalking them? She couldn't risk letting the kittens starve. Ysabel tried smuggling leftover food from her plate for the cats, but one of her little brothers loudly asked what she was doing, leading to an unpleasant look from the children's governess along with a lecture about how she needed to set a proper example for her siblings. After that, Cook set aside meat for the cats in the icebox, and when the rest of the family was asleep, Ysabel would steal downstairs, bring it out to the cats, and spend an hour or two with them. She enjoyed the cooler air and the noises of the night. If she strained her ears, she could pick out owl hoots and other animal sounds outside Tradetown. The kittens explored the kitchen yard. Every night, they became stronger, and their skills developed. Ysabel's anilink proved to be the most aggressive hunter despite his small size. She tried calling him Hunter a couple of times, but the name didn't seem suitable. Neither did Patch, Blackie, or even Link, which would have made her family ask some uncomfortable questions.

When the kittens were only a few days away from their two-moon birthday, the servants redoubled their housekeeping and cooking. The drapes were laundered with lavender and other fresh herbs, pressed, and rehung; all marks left by the younger children on the walls and floors were scoured off, and the best china and silverware were brought out of the safe and cleaned until they shone. Although Cook ordered fish, a roast, fine cheese, and berries, Ysabel got none of it.

"What's happening?" she asked after Cook dragged her into the broiling kitchen, then nearly lost her temper at the way Ysabel peeled the carrots.

"The Honored Lathatilltin is hosting a supper for his Silver Watch Society friends tonight," Cook replied. "He wants everything to be perfect, but he won't pay for extra help." She shook her head. "I need these pots cleaned now! Where's Hanna? Salth take that worthless girl!"

Ysabel lowered her head and pretended to focus on her work. The Silver Watch Society did more than support her father's business; they also worshipped Salth, the Goddess of the Dead Land near Tradetown. Salth was the ancient enemy of the Four Gods and Goddesses—and Their Avatars as well. She'd have to keep well hidden so they wouldn't notice her, but at the same time, she also needed to eavesdrop on them and learn their plans.

A pity I don't dare hide one of the kittens in the dining room. It can't be my anilink; he's too precious to risk, even if his hearing is better than mine. Maybe I can smuggle him upstairs and listen from above. Lathtin's room is right over the dining room, so we can hide in there.

Ysabel assisted in the kitchen for the rest of the day. She hung up her apron with relief when her mother summoned her to her private room.

"Thank the Four those men want nothing to do with us," her mother said as she rose from her pianoforte. "Ysabel, I want you safe up here so they don't see you. There's no need for you to help out in the kitchen. It's below your station anyway."

"Yes, Mama." *But how am I supposed to fetch my anilink?*

A bright mew sounded in her head. Her anilink sensed that she wanted him and obligingly waited by the kitchen door. As soon as Hanna opened it to pick more fresh herbs, he slipped inside the house.

By All Four, no! You'll get caught! Go back outside!

He didn't listen. He scampered across the kitchen floor, nails clicking against it. Ysabel held her breath, waiting for Cook to scream and throw a pan at the kitten, but she never turned around.

You'll never make it up the stairs, Ysabel told her anilink. *Hide near here.* She showed him an image of a dark corner near the servant's staircase. *I'll come find you.*

"Are you listening, Ysabel?"

"Mama, I …I have to go."

"By the Four, what are you doing?" Mama stood up from the pianoforte bench. "You need to stay hidden!"

"I'll hide. I promise." Ysabel darted for the door. "I just need to get something first."

Despite the urgency of her errand, she paused to check on Bethany's location. She wasn't in the hallway, but she could spring out from her room at the slightest sound. Taking care to step only on the worn carpet, Ysabel tread softly down the hall to the servants' stairs. She knew all of the creaky spots and shifted from side to side to avoid them. Once at the bottom, she stared at the corner where her anilink was supposed to wait. There was no sign of him.

Freeze that animal. Barely old enough to join me, and he's already causing trouble. Still, she couldn't help smiling. He was going to be a strong anilink. Now, if she could only discover a suitable name for him so she could call him. Instead, she was forced to walk up and down the dark hallway, mentally reaching for him and hoping he responded before she stepped on him. When she didn't find him, she opened doors to various rooms and storage closets. Eventually she found her anilink in a closet chewing on one of her brother's shoes.

"Freeze it, don't do that!" She scooped him up. "I can't let anyone else know you're here!"

Ysabel ran back up the stairs. This time she was less careful about making noise, and she winced when a step creaked. She hurried into Lathtin's room and sat against the door so Bethany couldn't barge in. The kitten prowled around her brother's room as if he'd known it all his life. *Maybe I should name him after Lathtin...no, that would be too confusing.*

"Go over by the window." She pointed at it. "Listen for me below."

The kitten explored for a few more minutes before he finally understood what she wanted. His tail twitched as he explored the wall for cracks. When Ysabel felt certain her sister didn't know where she was and wouldn't come looking for her, she joined her anilink. Touching his back help her link with his senses. She strained to listen for voices. Her own stomach growled in protest when she finally heard several pairs of footsteps entering the dining room, along with the clinks and clatters of the servants presenting the guests with food and wine. The guests murmured pleasantries to each other about the meal, the weather, and news from the capital of Wistica. Ysabel began to wonder if she would learn anything useful when her father said, "Yes, it's a pity about Lathtin. He had clever hands for watchmaking, even though he kept insisting he wanted to attend the University in Wistica and study medicine. I would have had a hard time making him change his mind, though I was thinking of threatening to marry off his twin sister if he didn't cooperate."

Ysabel shuddered. Her anilink jumped into her lap and licked her hand as if to comfort her. She reminded herself that no matter how horrible her intended husband would have been—Father would have deliberately chosen the worst possible match for her—Fall would have helped her escaped him.

"So, is she available?" another man asked.

Ysabel clamped down on the kitten, sending him a mute apology when he squealed.

"She'll need a great deal of discipline if you want to make a good Selathen wife out of her," her father said. "She's too much like her mother, wanting to think for herself instead of letting a man manage her properly. I should be grateful she's not as wild as Bethany. Ysabel would sooner feed the birds than look at a man. If she wasn't summer-born, I'd worry she was connected to the Challens' Fall Goddess."

Thank the Four my mother lied on my birth record to protect me.

"I've a mind to keep Ysabel close to home for now," her father said. "My next oldest daughter, Bethany, should be ripe for marriage in another two or three years. But if she's betrothed now, her intended will have time to mold her as he pleases."

The men traded ribald comments about Ysabel's sister while her ears warmed with their words. At least she was out of danger for now. Should she say anything to Bethany? Her sister might not even care.

"Married, Papa!" Ysabel started as Bethany's voice came through the wall. "Your friends are so old! They're not as handsome as—" She sighed.

Ysabel shook her head. Bethany had ideas above her station. As she stroked her kitten, she thought to him, *We must be very quiet. My sister is more likely to catch us than my father, but she'll cause more trouble than a gallon of fleas.*

The kitten snuggled against her, his sigh so faint Ysabel could scarcely feel it. He sent her trust and love so absolute it made her vision blurry.

They sat there for what felt like hours. Ysabel grew stiff from sitting on the floor, but she didn't dare move. The dinner continued below, but now she could also hear sounds from Bethany's room. Bethany paced for a while, then she was quiet. The kitten's sharp hearing caught faint scratches that could have been a pen on paper. Finally, creaks as Bethany struggled to open her bedroom window gave Ysabel and her anilink the opportunity to move without being heard.

Ysabel edged over to Lathtin's window. Instead of looking out herself, she held up the kitten to take advantage of his night vision. He was so small he fit on the windowsill easily without causing the drapes to bulge around him. It was still too early for Father's guests to be leaving;

he would offer them whiskey and cigars before they finally started talking business—and religion. What would draw Bethany to the window this late at night?

A moving shadow below caught the anilink's attention. A figure all in black stepped right underneath Bethany's window. Something white fluttered down next to him. He picked it up and set something small under a bush. The kitten tracked it all with the eagerness of a hunter.

Can you find that? Ysabel asked him. She worried he might be too small for the job and his mother would be a better choice, but he caught her thought and responded with indignation.

I do it!

Sometimes a mental link was a bad thing. The more she worried about him, the more he squirmed to get away. She finally sighed. *Be careful.* Ysabel kissed the top of his head before setting him down. She hurried to the door and opened it so the kitten could slip out. At the same time, Bethany's own door opened, and Bethany stepped out, a shawl around her shoulders.

"What's that?" She pointed at the kitten streaking away. "A rat! A rat! There are rats in the house!"

Ysabel restrained herself from swearing by the Four Gods and Goddesses of Challen. Her first thought was to deny the presence of rats, but then an idea came to her. "Well, where there's one rat, there's bound to be more," she said carelessly. As Bethany tried to get past her to the stairs, she mirrored her movements, blocking her sister. "Who knows, they could be in your closet right now spoiling all of your nice things."

Bethany's eyes widened, but she didn't dart back into her room. "You put rats in my room? I'm telling Papa for certain!"

"I never said or did any such thing, you silly goose! I'm just saying rats are social animals. They live together."

"No proper lady thinks so much about rats. No wonder Papa is having such a hard time marrying you off. How am I going to attend any balls or be courted if you're still unmarried?"

Ysabel spread her arms to block the narrow hall. "I think you're managing the courting part well enough on your own, Bethany."

Bethany tried to duck under Ysabel's arms, but she lowered them just in time.

"I don't know what you're talking about." Bethany's voice shook.

"Then why are you trying to get past me?"

"I...I...I need to go downstairs."

"Why?" Ysabel shouldn't be enjoying this as much as she was, but Bethany's behavior needed to be checked.

"I...I...I lost something!" Bethany let out a wail that would wake the children still in the nursery. "My glove! I must have dropped it outside."

"When?" Ysabel asked sweetly. "Before or after your young man stopped outside your window?"

She thought Bethany would crumple. For a heartbeat, her shoulders slumped. Then Bethany glared at her. "I don't know what you're talking about. You couldn't have seen anything."

Liar! Ysabel wanted to shout at her sister, but she couldn't risk explaining how she knew about Bethany's beau.

A faint mew caught her mental attention. Her anilink had been distracted by meat scraps in the kitchen and was busy devouring everything he could find. Cook had cornered him with an upraised broom.

"Freeze it!" Should she rescue her kitten and let Bethany retrieve her letter, or let her anilink suffer the consequences of his folly? Ysabel didn't have a choice; she would feel the kitten's pain too. "We're not finished," she told Bethany as she turned and raced down the stairs. Bethany followed. As Ysabel reached the bottom, Bethany pushed her and made her stumble. She fled in the opposite direction while Ysabel struggled for balance.

The only thing in her favor was that the kitchen was closer than the front entrance. Ysabel dodged around Hanna as she brought more plates into the kitchen. "Leave him alone, Cook!" she cried.

"Dama, it's a rat."

"It's not a rat; it's a kitten. He's doing no harm. Here, I'll let him out." Ysabel opened the kitchen door, and the kitten streaked past Cook to the outside. *Remember what you have to do,* she told him.

I know. I do!

She watched worriedly as the kitten raced around to the front of the house. Bethany was already outside, looking for the note. The kitten knew where it was and headed straight to it. Bethany spied his movement. With a longer stride, she beat him to the letter. She stopped to pick it up—

With a great bound, the kitten closed the gap. He pounced and pulled the letter away from Bethany, leaving only a corner of it in her grasp. *Ysabel, you see? I pounce!*

Yes. She smiled. *You're a great pouncer.*

Pouncer! I Pouncer!

Ysabel blinked. Her anilink had found his name. She didn't have time to rejoice, as Bethany chased Pouncer across the yard. The kitten dodged her and tore back to Ysabel. She stooped to pick him up, then she hid her sister's letter inside her sleeve.

Bethany, panting, found her. She pointed at Ysabel. "What did you do with my letter?"

"What letter? I thought you said there wasn't a letter."

"Well, that cat took it! I want it back."

"You can't have him." Ysabel held Pouncer closer. "He's mine."

"All I have to do is say something about him to Papa…"

"And then he'll find out about that letter you said wasn't yours. Maybe I'll even tell him you've been taking my belongings."

Bethany glowered at her, but Ysabel schooled her expression to stay calm. She'd defanged her sister now. Bethany might complain, but in the end, she would have to yield, like a dog that had lost a fight to another dog.

Bethany stomped back into the house. Ysabel scratched Pouncer behind his ear. *Do you want to come inside the house with me, or go back to your family, your mother and sisters and brothers?*

He pressed a velvet paw against her cheek. *You. You family.*

Smiling, she brought him back inside.

Jenna's Rosebush

As Jenna's seventeenth birthday approached, she was as skilled at turning a man's head as she was at turning a seed into a blossom. Yet although the men in her village were solidly built and pleasing to look at, none of them attracted her for more than a kiss and a feel behind the barn. None of them were the Spring Avatar she had been wedded to for more lifetimes than she remembered. This lifetime would surely be no different. All Jenna had to do was wait for Geoff or Grigor or Gareth— the Spring Avatar always had a name starting with "G," just as her name always started with "J" —to find her.

But it was hard to wait, with youth and appetite ready to burst out of her skin as if she too were a sprouting seed. Chaos Season had come several times during early spring, disrupting nature with snowstorms and heat waves. However, Jenna had kept the plants in her village from dying, and now they spread their leaves and blossoms in the warm sun. She too wanted to spread herself, to leave the little town of Bull Rock and travel around the country before settling down at the One Oak with the other Avatars of her generation. Instead, her father had her working in the fields with him from sunup to sundown, weeding and sowing.

"Once again, we'll have the best harvest in the village, maybe in the country, thanks to you, Jenna," he said one evening as they trudged home for dinner. "Why, we'll be the talk of the town!"

"The talk of the town?"

"Of course. And not just Bull Rock, but maybe all of Challen too!"

Father continued talking about his plans for the fields, but Jenna stopped listening. If her magic with plants attracted attention, maybe she could use it to let her Spring Avatar know where she was. She'd written once to the current group of Avatars asking when she could start training at their estate, but they'd said she would have to wait until the rest of her group could be located. Perhaps Jenna could use her plant magic as a signal. She could grow the biggest rosebush ever and let its scent perfume all of Challen. Her Spring Avatar would come and kiss her, and when they touched, all of the passion they'd felt for each other would reawaken. Then Jenna could live the life she was meant to live, the life of a Season Avatar.

* * *

Jenna already knew which rosebush she would pour her magic into. It grew near the well, and it boasted pure yellow roses, the color of the Goddess of Spring. Glory—that had been the Spring Avatar's name in her last life—would appreciate the gesture. All Jenna needed to do was find the energy to give to the bush. Thanks to growing up on a farm, she had plenty of experience using her magic. However, her father expected her to devote her magic to his crops, not to her personal projects. Even in spring, working on the farm drained her so much some nights all she could do was shovel as much food into her mouth as she could, then crawl into bed. It would take a miracle from the Four Gods and Goddesses to persuade her father to let her use her magic on the rosebush instead of the wheat. Could she arrange one on her own?

Before going to bed, Jenna held a twisted root from an oak tree. If she stared at it long enough, she could convince herself that it looked a little like a human figure. *God of Summer, help me do this. I know You and the rest of the Four expect us to look after this land for You, but I can't do it alone. I need to find the three Avatars from my generation, but I need to find the Spring one most of all.* She sighed. *I know we don't always get along, but that makes getting back together again that much sweeter. And I miss him. Surely the current group of Avatars are ready to rest now and let us take over. We usually switch when the youngest group is about twenty. I know we still have a few more years to go, but...it's so quiet in this town! Nothing ever happens here! All there is for me is just plants, plants, and plants. I need people too, Summer. I need my Spring Avatar. Please let him come soon.*

The root didn't respond. However, the next day, heavy rain ruined any chance they had at plowing. While Jenna's father mended tools and grumbled at the unexpected weather, Jenna slipped out into the storm before her mother could set her to churning or baking. Even with a waterproof cloak, Jenna quickly grew cold. But once she reached the rosebush, she squatted by the well for shelter and grasped the bush between the thorns. She closed her eyes and slipped into a trance. All she could feel were the roots in the ground and the leaves reaching for light. She sent magic into the plant, urging it to take the water and grow, to bloom, to release a wonderful scent. By the time her brothers found her, the rosebush soared as tall as the barn, with a root system equally deep.

"Jenna! Did you do that? What for?" Her oldest brother flinched as he pulled her away. "Ow! Next time you want flowers, pick something without thorns."

She groggily got to her feet and tried to brush the mud off of her dress. Her stomach complained as if she hadn't eaten in a moon. But as she examined her work, she couldn't help grinning. Roses bigger than her head were already blooming, and their scent drowned the air. The plant might not sustain itself without her magic, but it would last long enough for people to see and smell it. They would come and send word to the One Oak, to Wistica, to all corners of the kingdom of Challen. Then Jenna's Spring Avatar would come seek her out, and they'd be reunited.

***

As Jenna had hoped, her rosebush drew attention. Everyone in Bull Rock stopped by to see it—forcing Jenna's family to host a spontaneous gathering. Even though Jenna was the guest of honor, her mother insisted she be the one to hurry to the general store in town and purchase more sugar for baking and a couple bottles of wine. Jenna took a few quarter-chals from her hard-earned savings for green ribbons. When the Spring Avatar came to meet her, she needed to look her best.

The family farm was about an hour's walk from the town of Bull Rock. Jenna marked every clump of wildflowers she passed as landmarks. A bank of violets here, alfafa and clover over there, asters and bleeding hearts and bellflowers...before she grew tired, she'd reached Bull Rock. She tramped along the wooden sidewalk until she found the t'Reve's general store. A bell above the door tinkled as she stepped inside.

Jenna always enjoyed coming here, as the owner, Thomas t'Reve, was a master of arranging his wares into beautiful displays. Bolts of cloth and skeins of thread formed a rainbow along one wall, while cans of tinned vegetables had been stacked into a pyramid. Posters of fair-skinned women extolled virtues of finely milled and perfumed soaps, far fancier than the kind Jenna's mother made. The whole store reminded Jenna that Challen was so much bigger than Bull Rock. Many families had lived in this town for generations, never caring about the outside world. Not her. She was meant for bigger things. She was a seed that needed to fly far away from her roots. When would that happen?

Sir Thomas t'Reve bustled out of the storeroom with a crate of bottles. He was older than Jenna and not as well-muscled as the farmboys who flirted with her. In his favor, he had good teeth, a strong face, and more knowledge about the rest of Challen than all the other boys put together. He smiled when he saw her. "Jenna Dorshay! Always a pleasure to see you, Ava."

"I'm not an Ava yet," she reminded him. She couldn't help smiling herself. He was one of the townspeople who always remembered who she was destined to be.

He huffed as he set the crate down. "Everyone tells me your rosebush is the most beautiful thing they've ever seen in Bull Rock." He looked away and muttered something.

Jenna approached him. "I'm sorry. Did you say something?"

"It's nothing, Ava. I mean, Dama."

Perhaps he would be less flustered if he knew what to call her. Granting him permission to use her first name would have been very forward, not to mention giving him ideas of intimacy she didn't want to encourage. Jenna fumbled in her reticule. "Mama needs as much sugar as I can carry, and a couple bottles of—"

Sir t'Reve looked up at her, his face crimson. "You're the most beautiful thing in Bull Rock."

Caught by surprise, all she could do was raise her eyebrows.

"That's what I said earlier. Of course, I'm sure everyone else has already told you that by now."

"Just the boys," she managed to say.

"I'm not surprised they flock to you." For a moment, his expression was wistful, but he quickly smoothed it over. "Now, what else do you need besides sugar, Dama? Do you need any help bringing it back?"

Sir t'Reve hurried through the purchase as if he wanted to shoo her away. Yet, as he counted out her change, he hesitated before letting the quarter-chals fall into her hand. Their fingertips brushed. Jenna could have sworn his pulse throbbed in time with hers. Then he pulled away, his cheeks growing red.

"Thank you, Sir t'Reve. May the Four watch over you." Jenna left the shop before she remembered she hadn't picked out any green ribbons. She was too flustered to turn back.

By the Four, what just happened? He's not my Spring Avatar. He's not even as handsome as some of the other men in Bull Rock. Why would the merest touch of his make me feel drawn to him? Well, I'm not! Despite the heavy load of sugar she carried, she quickened her stride. *I can't be drawn to everyone I meet. There has to be a reason for it....*

The memory eluded her.

* * *

After the first celebration, people came from surrounding towns, even from Midpoint, the city closest to the Season Avatars' estate.

Jenna hurried over to the rosebush when she heard about the Midpoint visitors, hoping they were Avatars from the One Oak. She knew at once they were the wrong age, but she still smiled and flirted with them. Mama smiled and baked, but she didn't share the wine.

Half a moon passed, and the demands of spring planting kept everyone busy. The number of visitors dwindled, and Jenna soon only had time to check on her rose bush twice a day. Although she was tempted to make it grow even bigger, it was unsteady, rocking back and forth in the wind. The ground was bare around it, and all of the leaves on one side had turned brown. Perhaps she should prune it back down to its normal size. It wasn't worth leaching all the nutrients out of the soil for one bush, especially since it hadn't brought the Spring Avatar to her.

Jenna reached out to draw a branch closer to her. Before she could summon her magic, the sound of a heavy carriage being pulled by a team of belled horses reached her. What kind of traveler arrived with such fanfare? Perhaps the current Summer Avatar had finally come to take her away with him. Jenna rebraided her hair by feel. While a fellow Avatar ought to understand her desire to work with plants, she didn't want to be wearing one when they first met her.

High-pitched voices from the house shrieked with excitement. Jenna turned. What was happening? Should she go to the house, or wait here for the Avatar? She took a couple of step toward the house, but before she could get very far, her youngest sister, Clarie, ran to her.

Claire stopped running and held her side. "Ma says...come quick! There's a noble here for you!"

Jenna nodded. She'd thought so, but the confirmation still made her heart speed up. "The Summer Avatar?"

"No! Another one! Someone higher!"

"Higher than the Summer Avatar? The Spring Ava?" Spring Avatars tended to lead each quartet, but that never stopped Jenna from needling her Spring Avatar. Someone had to make up for his seriousness. But why had this Spring Avatar come for her instead of the Summer one?

"No, not a Season Avatar." Claire lowered her voice, and her eyes grew as big as sunflowers. "The Avatar of War."

Jenna bit back a laugh. The Avatar of War? That couldn't be. He wasn't part of the Season Avatars, and he didn't serve the Four Gods and Goddesses of Challen. The Avatar of War wasn't even from Challen. He was part of the Fip Dynasty, which had conquered Challen about four hundred years ago and added it to the Fip Empire. The Avatar of War was part of the royal family—the king's brother, if she remembered right.

"What would he want with me?" she couldn't help asking. Normally the Avatar of War ignored the Season Avatars. Jenna preferred it that way. The Four used the Season Avatars to keep Challen healthy and prosperous, despite the unpredictable appearances of Chaos Season and the drain on their food supplies to feed other parts of the Fip Empire. The Avatar of War, on the other hand, was more interested in helping his family conquer the world. Jenna wondered what he would do if he succeeded.

"What would I want with the upcoming Summer Avatar indeed?" a deep voice asked.

Apparently the Avatar of War hadn't waited for Jenna to come to him. He looked the part with his black jacket covered with medals. A touch of gray in his dark hair indicated he was older than he appeared. Although he was slightly stout and had a hooked nose, he held himself erect and confident. Jenna couldn't help staring. The farmboys around here might be stronger and younger, but they didn't have such power.

His expression shifted as he gazed at her. Jenna could tell from the way he leaned slightly forward that he found her appealing. *As well he should.* She licked her lips and smiled at him.

"I do not believe we have been properly introduced," the Avatar of War said. His cultured accent, so unlike the harsh way Jenna's neighbors spoke, made her skin tingle. "I am Lex ro Fip-Challen, Duke of Snoden."

Jenna sank into a curtsey, but it was hard to keep her gaze properly trained on the ground when she wanted to look at him.

"They say you're also the Avatar of War," she murmured, then added. "Your Highness."

"That's correct. That's why I also speak with the Season Avatars on behalf of my brother." His gaze lingered on her for a moment before moving beyond her. "And this must be the rosebush I've heard about. It is amazing." He glanced back at her. "But perhaps not the most amazing thing in Bull Rock."

Jenna felt her cheeks grow warm.

"Ava, will you walk with me for a bit?" He offered her his elbow, as if she was unaccustomed to walking on her home soil and wore delicately embroidered slippers instead of sturdy black boots. "I've come all the way from Wistica to see you, not your rosebush."

"Me?" Jenna tossed her hair, then, prompted by memories of etiquette from a previous life, rested her hand on his arm. "I didn't know anyone in the capital city would have heard of a farm girl like me."

He chuckled. "Ava, you obviously aren't just a farm girl. Someday you and the rest of your quartet will move to the One Oak and replace the current set of Season Avatars." He glanced around as if searching for a pretty place to walk with Jenna. But there was nothing here but fields and farms, all looking very much the same. "So, do you know where the rest of your group is?"

"Of course not. Your Royal Highness." If Jenna knew where the Spring Avatar lived, she could run away to be with him.

"Here in private, you may call me Avi. Or…."

Clarie stumbled, drawing attention to herself as she fell. She picked herself up before Jenna or the Avatar of War could. He narrowed his eyes as if wondering what to do with her.

"Clarie," Jenna said, "run to the house and ask Mama if we still have that bottle of wine."

"But—"

"It's quite all right, child," the Avatar said. "Your sister is safe with me."

Clarie made a face at Jenna before she turned around and left.

When she was out of sight, the Avatar glanced down at Jenna, smiling slightly as he squeezed her arm. "Do you really not know where the other Season Avatars are? I thought the four of you shared a special bond."

"Only the Spring Avatar can link with us, and we have to be touching for that to happen." Jenna's heart raced again.

"Where is he? Why don't you talk to him?"

"Talk to who?"

"The Spring Avatar."

The Avatar of War paused. "You didn't know the Spring Avatar is a woman this time?"

Jenna jerked away from him. "What! That's not possible!"

He watched her with a curious expression on his face. "I thought one of you was always a woman."

"That's the Fall Avatar, not Spring." She had trouble keeping herself from wringing her skirt. "Are you sure the Spring Avatar is a woman?" *It has to be a mistake. Please let it be a mistake.*

"I can't be absolutely sure until I meet her, or until she demonstrates her power publicly." The Avatar of War shrugged. "But there's only one spring equinox birth that's been registered with the Hall of Records in Wistica in the last twenty years, a young noblewoman, so from what I understand of how your gods work, she must be the one."

Maybe she's a Fallswoman in this life. Women who chose not to marry for whatever reason commonly dedicated themselves to the Goddess of Fall, just as their counterparts pledged themselves to the God of Summer. Could Jenna and the Ava Spring follow Fall when they already represented different deities? It didn't seem possible.

Does this mean we won't be together this time? He said she's noble. They often feel obligated to marry and have children. Maybe Gilna would still be willing to visit me in the middle of the night...

Jenna's head throbbed. Sometimes that happened when she remembered something new from her previous lives. She caught a glimpse of a fair-haired woman in an old-fashioned dress falling down a staircase. *Gilna's last death.* Guilt weighed in Jenna's heart. She was responsible, but she didn't remember how.

"Ava? Are you all right?" The Avatar of War knelt next to her, brushing his fingers over her cheek. She hadn't realized it was wet.

She stared at him without speaking. At this moment, he wasn't the Avatar of a foreign god, or the brother of her king. He was a man, a generation older to be sure, but still strong and powerful. If she couldn't have Gilna, then maybe he would do—at least for now.

"Hold me." Behind her, the rosebush extended sheltering branches around them. "Just ...hold me."

He raised his eyebrows. "Ava?"

"Call me Jenna." She forced a smile. Only a few layers of clothing separated them, and she could feel the heat coming from his body. No matter how mannerly he seemed, he still wanted her.

He stared at her for a few heartbeats, then bent his head to kiss her. She accepted him eagerly.

"Lex," he said when he broke away. He trailed a hand over her body, raising heat within her. Then he paused. "Your plant magic...there are ways a woman can use them so as not to get with child."

"I know them," she assured him as the roses cast shadows and sweetness over them both.

But your seed is too precious to poison. Expect it to bloom in nine moons.

* * *

A moon later, as Jenna struggled to keep her morning porridge down, she wondered if she ought to drink the special tea, the one that would kill the child she was certain she bore. What had she been thinking? The Avatar of War wasn't going to come back for her, even if he learned about the child. Her family soon would. Mama had examined the laundry more carefully than usual yesterday, as if she was mentally accounting for every item and knew Jenna hadn't used her moonflow rags recently. By the Four, Jenna didn't want to explain that.

She pushed her bowl away. "I'm going to walk the fields," she said. Ever since Jenna had come into her magic, she'd made a habit of patrolling her family's farm during the growing season. If she was close enough to plants, she could encourage desired ones to grow and prevent weeds from sprouting. She wasn't sure how effective she'd be if she felt ill, but at least she could figure out what to do while she walked.

Mama gave her a sharp look, but Jenna escaped before Mama could assign her chores around the cottage.

The air was starting to warm with true summer heat. Green in all its glorious shades gladdened her eyes. Although Jenna's bush sagged, it bore enough blooms to scent the air for miles around. She smiled as she passed it. She didn't regret the passion she'd shared with the Avatar of War. It was a shame she wouldn't be sharing it with the Ava Spring in this life—

She stumbled as a memory thrust itself into her mind: Glory falling down a staircase at the One Oak, breaking her neck. Glory's flight from Jenna's—or Jacob's, as she was known before—room a few heartbeats before, when she'd caught Jacob with another woman.

Oh! By All Four Gods and Goddesses, it was my fault. I shocked her to death. Jenna sighed. Maybe "shocked" wasn't the right word. For as far back as she could remember, she'd inevitably dallied with someone else when the Spring Avatar didn't spend enough time with her. No wonder Glory had said, "Enough!" and stormed out.

She won't be able to marry me, she won't become a Fallswoman for me, and, she won't want to have anything to do with me once she remembers the truth about her last death. Jenna hurried past the rose bush into a field of corn, but the stalks weren't tall enough yet to hide her.

How can I keep this from her? Is it even possible? Suddenly, the unborn child didn't seem like much of a concern.

Maybe one of the current Avatars can give me advice. The Avi Summer, perhaps, or even the current Ava Spring. Jenna grimaced. *I'll send letters to both of them and explain the whole thing. Maybe they'll allow me to live at the One Oak until our quartet is needed. I can figure out how to keep the truth from my own Spring Avatar.*

Now that she had a plan, Jenna forced herself to take deep breaths and focus on the crops. The corn was growing well, but some corn worms had gotten into part of the field. If Jenna was part of her full quartet, the Fall Avatar would have dealt with the pests in a heartbeat. On her own, the only thing Jenna could do was persuade the corn to do a better job of protecting itself, a more challenging solution than killing the corn worms outright or summoning birds to eat them. It took her several minutes to make the plants more toxic to their predators. By that time, Jenna felt nauseated again. She'd only covered a quarter of the farm, but she turned back to the house anyway.

Mama was shaping loaves of bread when Jenna returned home. Jenna hurried through the kitchen, but she halted when her mother looked up and said quietly, "Is there something you should tell me, Jenna Dorshay?"

She hesitated for a moment, pulling at her red braid, before saying, "I think I'm with child, Ma."

She sighed. "How many moons?"

"Barely a moon. It'll be a spring babe."

"If it lives. And you." Mama scattered flour over the table before looking at her with worried eyes. "The Four look after Their own, I suppose. I'm sure with the right tea and a prayer, Winter will aid you."

Jenna straightened up indignantly. "He most certainly will not!"

Mama stopped kneading to stare at her. "You plan to bear it?"

"Of course!" At least she'd have someone to help her remember her sweet encounter with War's Avatar—and someone to love her when her Spring Avatar turned away.

"It's already crowded enough in this house."

"How much room does a newborn need?"

"They grow faster than you think, and they cry at all hours of the day and night. Besides, William and his bride want to stay here while their new house is being built. There won't be room for a cradle."

Jenna raised her chin. "The One Oak has a nursery bigger than our house."

"So you say." Mama returned her attention to the dough. Normal people didn't retain memories of their previous lives, which made explaining Jenna's memories difficult. "Will the Avatars accept you with a child in your belly or arms?"

"They have to; I'm the only Summer Avatar of my generation." She tried to sound more confident than she felt. "I can still use my plant magic when I'm breeding or nursing, but I'll have to be careful not to use too much. It'll be easier when I join up with the rest of the quartet."

Mama pounded the dough against the table several times before dropping it back into the bowl. "And when will that be?"

"By the Four, I wish I knew." She put on a smile. "But I'm going to write to the current Avatars and ask them if I can move there now and wait for my quartet to arrive."

"What about the child's father? Will he be coming with you?"

Jenna's smile slipped. "I'll go write that letter."

"Jenna Dorshay! By All Four Gods and Goddesses—"

She hurried to the loft she shared with her sisters to borrow a sheet of paper and a quill from Cynta, who still attended school in Bull Rock. Cynta had run out of ink, but Jenna had made her own supply last year from blackberries. She wrote quickly, trying not to blot the page. "I need to come to the One Oak right away because...." A few drops fell on the paper as she thought. She wasn't comfortable telling the Avatars about her condition yet. It shouldn't matter what they thought of her. She hadn't hurt anyone by anticipating marriage. *At least, not this time...*

"Because I can't stay here a heartbeat longer!" The quill nearly tore through the paper as she wrote. She signed her name, folded the letter and sealed it with candle wax, then addressed it to the One Oak. After a few moments, she listed the Ava Spring as the recipient, not the Avi Summer. A woman would be more sympathetic to her plight.

Now all she had to do was bring the letter into Bull Rock to mail it. Jenna glanced down the ladder. Mama wasn't standing at the foot, but it would still be impossible to sneak past her. Luckily, Pa and Jenna's siblings arrived for lunch. Jenna hid her letter down her dress, then came down. She helped Mama bring in the dishes and food, just as she always did. Instead of taking her place at the table, she dashed out the door.

"By All Four, what ails her?" Papa said behind her.

She didn't linger to tell him. With the sun overhead, the air had warmed considerably from earlier. Although she loved the heat on her skin, her hair clung to her face. She paused to re-braid her hair before entering the town. The street was deserted, but Sir t'Reve waited patiently inside his shop. He smiled when she walked in.

"Ava, it feels like seasons have passed since your last visit. What can I do for you?"

"I'd like to send this to the One Oak." She slid the letter over the counter.

Sir t'Reve stared at the address for several heartbeats without touching the letter. "Does this mean you've been summoned away from us?"

Jenna sighed and wished that was true. "Not yet."

He pulled out a postage map to calculate the distance between Bull Rock and the One Oak. "We're fortunate to keep you in our town for a little while longer, then."

Jenna wondered what would happen when she started to show. Most people—except those dedicated to Summer and Fall—married before having children. Everyone in Bull Rock knew she was the next Ava Summer. Only the royal family ranked higher than the Season Avatars, so the farmers and townspeople wouldn't dare say anything to her face. That wouldn't stop them talking about her on the other side of the tree, though. She squared her shoulders. *Let them talk.* Their disapproval would make all the sweeter when she deigned to return in a gown and jewels worthy of her rank.

"Something wrong, Ava?" Sir t'Reve reached under the counter, but as he straightened, he wheezed.

"I should be asking you that question." She studied him for a few heartbeats. The Ava Spring was a matchless healer, but Jenna could treat some illnesses with plants.

Sir t'Reve gasped for breath for many heartbeats, long enough for Jenna to worry. His lips turned blue, but he waved away her offers to help. He sank onto a stool and strained to recover his breathing.

"Nothing...to...worry...about...Ava." He watered some wine and offered it to her before draining the cup. "It happens every so often."

"You should travel to the One Oak and ask the Ava Spring to examine you."

He smiled wryly. "My parents took me there when I was a child. The Spring Avatar said my lungs are fine."

Jenna humphed. The Avatar must not have checked him thoroughly. "I'm certain my Ava would be able to help you."

"It would be an honor to meet her." Sir t'Reve jumped up and studied the postage map. "It's a half-chal for regular post. If you want it to go express, that's a full chal."

Right now, she couldn't spare a full chal. The sooner she escaped her parents' questions, the better. "What if I gave you a half-chal now and brought you herbs for a tea?"

"A tea blend to sell?"

"No." She looked straight at him. "Just for you."

His eyes widened. "I...would like that very much."

Their gazes met. To Jenna's surprise, her cheeks grew warm. She finally had to break the eye contact by turning to the skeins of locally-spun yarn for sale. She chose a soft yellow one, since she expected her child to be born in the spring. "I'll bring more items in to trade for this," she promised.

As she walked home, she clutched the yarn to her chest and wondered what was wrong with her. Imagine finding herself interested in the plain, unassuming local shop owner! Once she was recognized as Summer Avatar, the most handsome and richest noblemen would plead for the chance to court her. She could flirt with them and act as if she chose first one, then another, breaking all their hearts along the way.

Jenna stopped in the middle of the dirt path. She'd done similar things in every life she could remember. What had it done for her? Yes, she'd enjoyed pleasures and partners beyond imagining, but no matter how much she used others to get her Spring Avatar's attention, it never worked out well. Jealousy, arguments, anger so deep it infected the rest of the four-fold link, a sudden death, and now a lifetime of linking with an Avatar who would never marry her or become a Fallswoman for her. Yet again she was on a path that would take her away from happiness. How could she change and be what her Spring Avatar deserved?

She glanced up as a morning dove called to her. Maybe Sir T'reve, as unlikely as it seemed, had something to teach her.

* * *

For the next quarter-moon, Jenna drank mint tea and nibbled bread crusts as soon as she rose in the morning. Her stomach issues didn't disappear, but they became more manageable. She did her best to help Ma in the morning and Pa in the afternoon, though despite all her offers, they didn't send her on an errand into town. In the evening, when she might have otherwise drifted down to Bull Rock to dance and listen to music, she collected every plant she thought might help Sir t'Reve. She dried bunches of lavender and tied them with ribbon or made sachets. After the rest of the family went to bed, she knitted baby hats and mittens for her babe.

One afternoon, as she was chopping vegetables for soup, her youngest brother went upstairs to change and came down wearing one of the hats. "Mama, are you having another baby?" he asked.

Mama shook her head. "Thank the Four I'm getting too old for that."

"Then who is it for?"

Jenna was spared an awkward explanation by a knock on the door. "I'll get it," she called. As she wiped her hands on a towel, she wondered who it was. A neighbor seeking her plant magic? Someone for her parents? It had been a while since one of the local youths called on her, and they were likely still working in the fields. Perhaps it was someone from the One Oak sent to bring her back. Her heart quickened at the thought.

Disappointment flared in her when she saw Sir t'Reve, but only because she had half-convinced herself it had to be someone from the One Oak. His face was flushed, and she wondered if he'd had more problems breathing on the trip. She smiled at him. "By the Four, Sir t'Reve, I don't believe I've ever seen you outside of the store before."

He gulped for air before answering her. "I don't actually live there, you know."

"How was your walk?" Belatedly, Jenna remembered her manners and opened the door wider. "Won't you come in and have something to drink?"

Mama took over, fussing over the last of the wine before realizing it had gone bad, then having Jenna fetch more beer from the cellar. Sir t'Reve responded politely to Mama's questions, but he watched Jenna the entire time. He sipped his beer, then brought out a letter. "This just arrived today, Ava. As soon as I saw where it was from, I knew you'd want to see it right away."

The One Oak! Jenna could tell it was from there by the fine linen paper and proper wax seal, complete with the One Oak insignia. She scanned the address for the name at the bottom. *Dorian Gran Garnell, Avi Winter. Why would he respond to me?* She wanted to tear the letter open, but with other people watching her, she used a clean butter knife instead. As soon as she skimmed the words, she wished she'd waited to read it privately. Now there was nothing she could do but put on a brave face.

"The Avi Win says I have to wait until I'm needed, just like every other Season Avatar since the first quartet," Jenna said.

Mama sighed. "And no word when that'll be?"

"It could be next moon, next year, or five years for now. Only the Four know for certain, and They never tell us."

Mama patted her hand and rose. "Don't fret, Jenna. We'll figure something out."

As Mama started washing up, Sir t'Reve leaned forward and whispered, "What does she mean? If you don't mind me asking, that is."

Jenna's stomach grumbled. She wished Mama had offered their guest food along with something to drink. Even bread and cheese would have been welcome. The berries out back ought to be ripe by now. They'd have more privacy back there.

"Did you ever have a chance to see the rose bush I grew?" she asked.

He shook his head.

"Then you should come with me before you head back. It's not as spectacular as it used to be, but it's still worth seeing."

Sir t'Reve set his beer down and followed her. He grinned as soon as he stepped outside. "By the Four, how did I miss smelling that earlier? It's as if you have all the roses in Challen, Ava!"

She smiled and didn't correct him.

They followed the rose-scented breeze back to the barn. The once-proud bush sagged under the weight of all its flowers. The few leaves still visible were brown-spotted, and Jenna could detect a faint odor of rot beneath the perfume. She'd been so busy with other things lately that she'd neglected her creation, and now it was dying. What had once seemed like a brilliant idea now was nothing more than a foolish waste of space and water. Nevertheless, Sir t'Reve gawked at it as if he'd never seen an Avatar's magic before. He paced up and down in front of it, then stroked the petals of a flower. "Ava, would it presume too much to gather some fallen petals as a memento?"

"No, of course not. Here." Jenna deftly separated roses from their stems. "You may have as many as you like."

The wonder in his face transfigured him. For a moment, Jenna could imagine Sir t'Reve as the shy God of Summer, unable to participate in earthly pleasures but delighting in the joy they brought people. She might not miss many people from Bull Rock once she left, but she realized she would miss him.

"I wish you could come with me to the One Oak." The words were out of her mouth as soon as she thought them.

Sir t'Reve's eyes opened wide. "Me, Ava? How could I? I have a shop here to run. What would I do at the One Oak?"

She looked at him for a long moment. "You could be my husband."

His face flushed so she feared for his health. Bringing him to the One Oak and her Ava Spring's attention might be the best thing she could do for him.

"By All Four Gods and Goddesses, Ava—"

"No, don't say anything. At least, not yet." She took a deep breath. "I'm with child, Sir, t'Reve. The father…he doesn't know and likely never will."

"So, you need me to pretend to be the child's father."

As soon as he spoke, Jenna realized how much she'd insulted him. "No, no, that's not necessary! I mean, some people may care, but there's nothing they can do about it since I'm the next Summer Avatar, is there?" She reached for him. "Forgive me for saying anything. I just greatly admire you—" she couldn't say she loved him; that was a gift for the Spring Avatar alone—"I admire you so much it would be an honor to be Jenna Dorshay t'Reve."

"By All Four Gods and Goddesses." He smiled now. "The honor is all mine, and it would be if you were a Season Avatar or no." He took her hand. "I will take you, Jenna, if you will take me."

"By All Four—" she flushed. "I don't even know your first name."

"Thomas."

"Thomas." The word tasted as sweet as roses. "Then let us be wed."

She leaned forward and let him kiss her. As their lips met, her arm tingled. Despite the distraction, they lingered in the kiss, tasting each other, before Pa shouted something at them.

Thomas pulled away and placed himself between Jenna and her father. "Good sir, Jenna and I are celebrating our betrothal—"

"No," she said with more serenity than she felt. "Our wedding."

She drew back her sleeve. Blue script, too ornate for any mortal tattoo artist to duplicate, appeared above her wrist: TtR. Thomas stared at his initials for several heartbeats before displaying his own arm. Only two letters—JD, for Jenna Dorshay—appeared there in green, but they looked as elegant as the ones Jenna now bore.

Jenna traced her marriage tattoo with a finger, but it felt as if it had always been part of her skin. She hadn't expected the Four to bless this marriage so obviously, but it reassured her.

"By All Four Gods and Goddesses." Pa took off his straw hat and wiped his forehead. "Who marked the pair of you, and when did you have it done? Dame a'Brun can't ink anyone like that."

"It wasn't her. It was the Four, just now." Jenna's hand trembled until Thomas took it. "They approve the match."

Pa stared at her for a moment, his eyes wide. Ordinary humans seldom saw such direct evidence of the Four. Finally he hugged first Jenna, then Thomas. "Welcome to the family, townie." He slapped Thomas on the back. "You take good care of her, or I'll hitch you to the plow."

"Papa!"

Shaking his head, Papa hurried toward the house, yelling, "Ma! Kill the old hen for dinner! We have a surprise!"

Jenna and Thomas would only have a few more moments of privacy before her family swarmed her. She pulled him close for another kiss. His heart stammered in his chest. No, she would never be able to link with him the way she did with her Ava Spring, and he wasn't an impressive specimen like the Avatar of War, but Thomas still felt solid and loyal in her arms. Perhaps he could be her Avatar of a new kind of love, someone to teach her how to be a better person. Sharing the One Oak with him and asking her Ava Spring to heal him was the least she could do in return.

"Come with me." She guided him past the rose bush to a grassy bank out of sight of the farmhouse. "Let's celebrate the season while it's here."

Other Works by Sandra Ulbrich Almazan

Science Fiction: Catalyst Chronicles Series

Lyon's Legacy
The Mommy Clone
Twinned Universes
Seasonal Stories from the Sagan

Non-Fiction

Life at Seventeen Syllables a Day: A Journal in Haiku
SF Women A-Z: A Reader's Guide

Fantasy: Short Stories

The Book of Beasts
Letters to Psyche
Silver Rain

Fantasy: Season Avatars Series

Seasons' Beginnings
Scattered Seasons
Chaos Season
Fifth Season
Summon the Seasons
Young Seasons: A Season Avatars Short Story Collection
Season Avatars Complete Box Set

About the Author

Sandra Ulbrich Almazan started reading at the age of three and only stops when absolutely required to. Although she hasn't been writing quite that long, she did compose a very simple play in German during middle school. Her science fiction novella *Move Over Ms. L.* (an early version of *Lyon's Legacy*) earned an Honorable Mention in the 2001 UPC Science Fiction Awards. Her short stories have been published in two anthologies (*Firestorm of Dragons* and *MCSI: Magical Crime Scene Investigation*) and in the webzine *Enchanted Conversations.* Other works include the science fiction *Catalyst Chronicles* series, the fantasy *Season Avatars* series, *SF Women A-Z: A Reader's Guide*, and several science fiction and fantasy short stories. She is a founding member of Broad Universe, which promotes science fiction, fantasy, and horror written by women. Her undergraduate degree is in molecular biology/English, and she has a Master of Technical and Scientific Communication degree. She's currently a QA Representative; she's also been a technical writer, a part-time newspaper, copyeditor, and a lab tech. Some of her other accomplishments are losing on *Jeopardy!* and taking a stuffed orca to three continents. She lives in the Chicago area with her husband, Eugene; and son, Alex. In her rare moments of free time, she enjoys crocheting, listening to classic rock (particularly the Beatles), trooping as a Jawa or Imperial Officer with the Midwest Garrison of the 501st Legion, and watching improv comedy.

Sandra can be found online at the following links:

Website (www.sandraulbrichalmazan.com)

Blog (www.ulbrichalmazan.blogspot.com)

Twitter (@ulbrichalmazan)

Facebook (https://www.facebook.com/SandraUlbrichAlmazanSffAuthor)

Goodreads (http://www.goodreads.com/author/show/5282664.Sandra_Ulbrich_Almazan)